Child of illusions

Written by
Camillia Mahal

ISBN: 9781689263207

CHILD OF ILLUSIONS

CAMILLIA MAHAL

I wear a lot of masks and identities.

I am a million little souls living in a million different places with millions of random experiences—all within a moment, encapsulated in one body.

This book has not been written by me, but rather through me. From the source through the cosmos, which then channelled my crown chakra to this paradise called Earth.

TABLE OF CONTENTS

GRATITUDE

I would like to thank the universe for bestowing upon me the biggest present: the gift of life. For all of my experiences that have shaped me into what I am and what I am to become.

To my mother, who showed me a world of magic and love, as well as how to follow my heart no matter what pain I may endure. I love you. To my father, for bestowing wondrous mystics upon me and showing me how to find my way to seek truth within.

To my animals, who have taught me how to find love through compassion and unconditional love. Thank you for being my guides.

To all who I have encountered, no matter how small or long our journey has been, from the critters to those who walk with skin, thank you for shaping my universe in every form that you have.

May the gods always bless those in existence.

एक

"Death may be the greatest of all human blessings."

– Socrates

I've been here many times. I keep reincarnating into the energy of everything that can, has, and will exist. I was born for a reason that became lost as my life unravelled. So, I started to seek the meaning of life.

Who am I? What am I? Why am I here?

Why do I keep coming back in so many different costumes?

As a child I recalled past-life memories vividly and spoke of them with my mother. I began to face my fears as a young child, examining my soul and where thoughts and blocks came from (and why they lived in me even after all these lifetimes). I came to see that as much as I loved and lived life, I was still scared of death.

I was petrified of the unknown.

I was scared of myself, the invisible spirit within.

If I didn't face these thoughts, they would continue and lurk within every birth. I don't want to keep coming back to this dimension. I'm on one of my last births…maybe the last.

But at times, I still live in this human body, which is attached to an ego and this material plane of existence. And the face of fear still lurks in the shadows behind the curtains that I cannot see.

I look like a panther, maybe that's why people are intimidated by me. Most fear wild, unpredictable animals—not to mention my feline etiquette. Wild energy and wisdom speak through my eyes. Many try to label me—maybe in pure confusion because of my complexity and spontaneity.

Even I'm baffled at times.

I'm a captivated nun in a bad girl's body: dangerous to most, as I'm unpredictable. On a whim I find my way to cartels in Colombia because of a book I've read, and then in another instant I transform and become one of many faces on a film set. Walking with so many lifetimes in one body, my temple is addicted to experiences and transformations.

I'm 38 and have a midnight mane that flows down my back and a few tattoos. My first tattoo was the kanji for "death" in Japanese on my neck, which I got with a drug dealer when I was 17. I had odd dreams after getting it about samurais and extreme deaths that kept me up most nights. I got the kanji for "life" later, learning balance and patience amidst the chaos.

I also have "Maktub" in Arabic on my right wrist, which means "your destiny is written," as well as an Abraham Lincoln quote on my forearm, which reads "this too shall pass" (from his famous speech). Every tattoo was inked in the moment. I have no regrets. I live spontaneously through the universe.

I was born a chameleon.

It all began when the celestial conduits toyed with the cosmic forces before I was born. I remember seeing my parents before I took this birth. Many battles were fought to see if it would come to fruition. I chose my parents, Paul and Sylvia, because of who they were and where their seeds originated from. A lineage of destinies constructed by the stars.

I was conceived at the Tropicana Hotel in Las Vegas. A little lower budget than my past life's regal ways, but I'm adjustable. Palm trees lined the beautiful blue sky of the desert. I loved the sounds of slot machines and the bright lights, the juxtaposition of bells and old desert air. When my mother told my father she was pregnant, he thought it might be best to exterminate me—understandably so because of their chaotic, abusive, and broken marriage.

I felt copious amounts of tension and pain as I curled up hidden in her supposed pouch of protection, wondering what I got myself into. There were many times I had to leave her stomach, as I couldn't handle the unbearable anxiety. I was an escape artist, which later led to deadly habits. Eating ample amounts of sugars until I was numb and sick was one of my first addictions, which developed into deathly addictions as an adult.

I did everything I could to disappear.

My mother took herself to the hospital when she went into labour. She hailed a cab because my father couldn't have bothered or cared; he had to be called to make an appearance by my godmother. And when he arrived, he told everyone they were missing the "trill" of it all, not the thrill.

I was born at 11:01 a.m. on August 24th, 1980.

I elicited such confusion and mystery that I was left nameless. From my first breath, my father called me Princess, even though I was never treated like one. When one is left nameless, they can become anything—a shapeshifter, as the energy vibrates to the conscious and unconscious, visible and invisible. My mother found it comical when she was threatened with fines at her government job for not naming me.

I was left without an identity for six months.

One morning it came to her when she was taking the trash out. Of all things, she looked down at a paper garbage bag that read **Camillia**. Immediately, she picked up the phone and called my godmother.

"Is it Camillia with a K or C?"

In a very proper English accent, my godmother Myra replied, "Camillia." I was then known as Camillia Sunita Mahal. Camillia means "helper to the priest" in Latin. Sunita was Buddha's first disciple, who was so poor that he discovered unlimited riches within: he found his soul and therefore became enlightened. Mahal in Arabic means "palace" and is the epitome of love.

Sylvia's (my mother) real name is Lakshmi—named after the Hindu goddess of riches and luxury. "Lachhammi" is tattooed in purple on my left wrist, purposefully misspelled because of her mother's spelling. A beautiful disposition, a refined love of the arts, and an eye that could find invisible details frames her beautiful soul. From *The Jungle Book* and

1001 Arabian Nights to the crying in the washroom, something in her fairy, whimsical world called to me.

My mother's father was a charming mobster, known as the "Hindu godfather" for his horrific, but lucrative illicit acts—from pimping to murder. Her Tibetan mountain mother was a woman of envious beauty who experienced great depths of pain and struggle even though she achieved monumental achievements in business and film.

She was also born under a magical spell.

My mother's brother, Tab, jammed with the Beatles and opened for Ike and Tina Turner—and was a wonderful horse wrangler. That's where my love stemmed from. He even taught me about astral projection and meditation. He was mystical; yet, he was too sensitive for the world. He didn't know how to channel his energy so it wouldn't take him over. In the end, I buried him alone in a ceremony with the invisible forces.

Moments like that test your faith of inner strength.

Her older sister, once prim and proper, ran away, married questioningly, and then became a devout Jehovah's Witness. An odd set of marbles, though I appreciated that. She had a handful of half-brothers and sisters who were of all sorts. Addictions, love, talent, and danger ran through their passionate veins. Generations of souls made of the rarest concoctions of forces.

My mother had my sister from her previous marriage. I adored Romina. She would put me in a sock basket as she did the laundry while Michael Jackson's "Thriller" album played in the background. I loved watching *Dynasty* with her.

I knew my brother from a past life; my mother had him with my biological father. He was angry and dark from the very beginning—another reason I was scared to enter into this karmic dysfunction.

द्वौ

As a child I asked the gods to make my life as difficult as they could so I could experience what others go through and what the world was. Maybe because I walked in so many shoes and lifetimes before that I wanted to experience the richness of life through many different perspectives. I thought I would never know why I asked for such a fate; until one afternoon while I was writing this novel I read a book that had the answer. It said:

> "Souls who are on their way home to the heavens choose to take births where they can experience all that they can, where they have inner memories from previous births. They do this so that they can walk in an endless amount of journeys, to help everyone they can, for they speak to another heart from their own, they have become a clearless quartz that reflects all—which allows them to be transparent, to reflect what is—so withered souls can grow and continue with inspiration in their profound journeys."

At the age of five, I asked my mother why she married my father, telling her about his uncountable affairs even though I never saw them. I was born psychic. I could feel everything. I didn't need to see to know. She always brushed me off, wondering where I found such knowledge without proof.

How could a child know?

Ignorance is bliss.

I saw violence and rage in my daily life; so much so, that I couldn't be certain anything safe existed—even in my imagination. My innocent eyes had been robbed. This went on for eight more excruciating years.

I was thirteen when I asked my father to go for a drive in his 1993 steel-grey Honda Accord. In between one of our many bouts of silence, I finally asked him why he stayed and created chaos in the lives around him. Why not choose to live the life that one really wants? He left, but the struggle continued on: From no food in the fridge because of my father, who refused to pay child support, to my brother, who had now taken my father's violent behavior and inflicted it upon me daily.

My father moved back to India with his latest affair, his music teacher. It ended before it truly began. He built a home in Mahal village that looks like a miniature Taj Mahal, surrounded by lush, unkempt gardens and the sounds of wild creatures.

Cobras slither by and make love before your eyes.

He can create unbelievable things—a mad genius in many ways. He can build a solar home and a lumber mill in Siberia from scraps, harvest the gardens, and solve the most complicated math equation in his mind while having a conversation about the deep intrinsic mysticism of the universe.

I never know what energy I will enter into or what I'm going to feel in his energy.

It's always a surprise within a surprise.

Perhaps a visit to the Himalayas, where I stumble upon a Sadhu who prepares for his death with a gravesite that he has dug as he requests I massage his dreadlocks daily with ashes——or pondering life's irony in my *Looney Tunes* onesie PJs in the middle of nowhere on his scooter with wild Indian jaguars prowling the black of the night. We connect in a way that makes me want to strangle him, but, at the same time, laugh uncontrollably as I see myself in him. Some of my experiences with him are so disastrous I often questioned why I have him in my life, and if I would even see him again. Other times, I feel as though an omnipresent force of God has been exposed through our experiences.

I was in my twenties when I professed my profound fear of being attached to my body and my mind that I was now a servant to. Death captured me; life became unknown. Experiences, life, habits, pains, and sadness caged me. Life had secretly left so many invisible markings on me.

I yearned so deeply to connect to Mother Earth. I needed to dance again with the universal consciousness, unconditionally, where I didn't have to think with my mind and where my body would know, like when I was a child.

When I was free.

He advised me to walk around the open gravesite in the village daily. I was told that I had one purpose, and that was to let go of my attachment of what I will never own—my illusionary mind. In his very Indian accent, my father spoke of how the mind lives in the past and future, but hardly in the present, for that takes a disciplined mind that is centered and man strays far from that. Man can't control his mind; therefore, he runs, up, down, and all around because he can never master the center, the mind. Therefore, he has no knowing of self.

At first, I was perplexed as to how this would help me overcome my fear of death. My mind persisted. As is often credited to Einstein: "Insanity is thinking the same thing over and over again and expecting a different result." This is what most brains do. Truly, a human rat wheel. It sounded morbid, but that was another issue he spoke of. I lived with fear, judgement, and labels; that closes an open door. I later learned that Buddha taught this technique to his disciples who feared death and meditation.

I started walking ritualistic, never-ending circles around the wooden planks atop a cement plank—an amalgam of dust, ashes, and souls. The willow tree and open shrine were dedicated to the gods, showing its omnipresence with the heavenly incenses that burned.

I sought answers within the leftover bones and skulls, wondering who they belonged to and where they went. I was fascinated by darkness and light—the duality of life. I held the bones in my hands and watched as life was spoken through death. Daily, I watched anonymous bodies burn and slowly I began to visualize myself burning within the fire. I cried to the universe through my unspoken words, wondering who I was, where I was, and what I was to become.

I am a temporary visitor in a temple that I occupy until my last breath. When and how, or where it ends, I do not know. All that is experienced is my manifestation and visualization of thought and energy.

There is no true death; that, too, is an illusion.

No beginning and no end.

No birth, no death.

त्रय

Every morning I am awoken by a beautiful aroma that lingers throughout the village into my bedroom window from a mint farm across the way. I bow before the god of light, the Hindu god Surya, and my beloved Egyptian god, Ra. My mornings usually begin with walking with invisible forces on feeding quests.

I am obsessed with feeding the divine—sometimes up to 12 hours a day in the scorching summer days. Sweat profusely drips down my spine; the taste of salt leeches into my mouth as my palm stays open to feed all that I can. I don't stop until it is dark, when the stars and strays have followed me home and my face has been stained with laughter and tears. The humans know I will be back. Every night I go to sleep with the most beautiful orchestra directed by wild and exotic birds that reside and visit my father's oasis.

But this morning was not like the rest.

A sudden thirst for a glass of freshly squeezed mango juice seized me. I advised my father of my desire and we hopped onto his scooter and glided through the planet's vision of a new dawn. The juice stall, if you could call it that, was a short trip away, a mere twenty minutes. But twenty minutes in India yielded trillions of worlds for the eye to feel and behold.

Our regular juice wallah set up his bike stand, where he served his daily customers wearing tattered kurta pajamas and a loosely tied paisley turban. His freshly squeezed mango juice was heavenly—perfection in a cup. I watched as the courageous street dogs of India crossed the streets as vendors set up their stands. I downed two more glasses and looked at my father, which was a sign that I was done. I complimented the juice vendor on his artistry and left a generous tip.

The freedom you feel gliding through the air in India is surreal. You feel as if you are flying. You become so still within that you become like air and embrace the nothingness of the universe. And that is when I could hear the inner messenger. And it spoke, "Pull over onto Gt Road, the ancient dirt road that has connected all of India since the beginning of time."

"Pull over, Pauli. Please."

It was a nickname I bestowed upon my father, Paul Mahal. His given Indian name is Amarjit Singh Mahal—like the Sikh Singh warrior he is, but fervently denies. I looked across the dirt road and saw some pundits—also known as seers, mystics, or forecasters to the stars. My parents don't openly believe in psychics, especially my father, but they always listen curiously and mindfully. It made sense, as my mother's grandparents and parents dabbled in the supernatural and performed many ritualistic rites. They could conjure up all sorts of herbal medicinal concoctions and spellbinding magical recipes.

I saw at least five or six lithe pundits laying down on a small patch of cement across the freeway sweltering in the hallucinating summer heat. They were wrapped in light shawls and contorted in yoga poses; an air of sloth and magic mixed into mysticism. I didn't even need to glance at them to know which pundit mine was. He sat in his white kurta pajamas just like the rest, but I never chose "just like the rest."

There was something special about him and his demeanor, something extraordinary, out of the ordinary. In front of him on the dirt floor was a small, worn book with a faded green cover. Food trails covered his kurta pyjamas, leaving proof of what he ate: vegetable curry, from maybe well over a year ago, and oil stains that spoke of his deep love of coconut desserts. His white flowing beard reminded me of a mythical god as the sun shone upon him, even more so because of the majestic beauty he exuded.

We immediately locked eyes.

His deep-seated cat eyes never glanced away as soon we made eye contact. Neither did mine as I walked into his soul. He slowly started to rise while remaining on his side, as if he were levitating. He uncoiled like a snake, trying to straighten what he could of his worn turban. I looked behind him and saw a beautiful park with green peepal trees, bodi trees, and blossoming fruit trees. The evergreens reached thirty meters and bore small figs. It reminded me of a story I heard about Vishnu and how he took a birth under this noble creation.

I sat in child's pose, watching as he watched me.

After some silent breaths, he started to speak Punjabi. My understanding of the language is good enough to get me by for the simple things in life, but not enough to comprehend my future destinies and complicated past lives. I understand much more by silent expressions and feelings.

I indicated to my father that I needed a translator, meaning him. I told him to relay what the pundit said without his ideas and perceptions of what was being said. My father likes to misconstrue others for his own sense of entertainment and the joy he derives from pushing boundaries. He also loves to add his own stories so he feels included and maintains relevance in his mind.

He must have been my court jester at one time.

Kabir, the seer, started speaking of the usual things: marriage and what my prospective husband would be like. Seers since the beginning of dawn were sought by Indian families to learn about their daughter's future marriage prospects. It was quite odd to hear this, as my father always told me to avoid the disaster of marriage.

I watched as he opened a dilapidated tissue, which held some shiny gems to ward off sicknesses or to produce riches––pearls, crystals, and stones of semi-precious quality. Some of them were obvious imitations. He never tried to sell or even properly showcase them. He revealed how I suffer mild stomach ailments due to my anxious soul, back then and now. "Her Virgo stomach holds many earthly feelings she hasn't let go of from her past births."

He pointed his finger between his eyes and tapped his third eye. Inhaling deeply, he spoke. "Her imagination is like no other. This is gifted from the gods. Created just for her, just like her rare existence. One day, she will tell of all the tales that she has lived."

I slide my hand on top of his, dying to feel our connection once again. His dry weathered hands melted into my palms as I remembered the familiarity. His mouth cracked into a crescent moon that acknowledged my knowledge.

And then he spoke the words I waited an eternity to hear. "One day, she will be back with the king."

I couldn't let go of those words.

Back with the king…back with the king.

I didn't inquire more.

There was nothing to say.

I stood up and gracefully placed my hands over Kabir's feet in gratitude. I bowed in prayer and thought: *Lucky me, destiny has aligned again; the stars have spoken.* We parted like ghosts—without looking at one another.

चत्वार

T he Mughal dynasty was known as "India's Golden Age." Philosophy was revered and the arts flourished. Exquisite opulent dynasties began with King Babur and bled into the current architecture. Artists were demi-gods who painted the most exquisite and unique backdrops upon the most magical and majestic sacred sights. Each utterance and stroke of art sought divinity. My favourites were ornate murals with inscriptions of universal love painted upon the snow-white domes of temples. When the sun gleamed, all was reflected in the sky. We were storytellers who used every medium possible for self-expression. It was a world where what you expressed and exposed was what lived in your soul— —the raw vulnerability of truth.

Akbar the Great was declared the king of all kings. As Babur's grandson, he assumed the throne amidst an unstable government surrounded by rivals at 13. When Akbar's father, Humayun, fled his kingdom, the only thing he took with him was 150,000 manuscripts on camel. Akbar's tolerance and intellectual pursuits were world-renowned. His thirst was unquenchable; his need for truth was the blood that ran deep in his veins. He never "sought" answers of earthly life. After all, gathering information for an answer is placing expectations and attachments to an outcome; in doing so, you miss the spontaneity and beauty of the surprise called life. His compassion for humanity was humbly noble.

He never showed favoritism.

The true source of power behind the Mughal reign was that everyone believed in a source higher than the self. It was spoken how death would be avoidable if they held such infinitesimal powers and how the karmic laws of the gods were very different than those made by man. Akbar was so connected to the divine that he saw his face in everything that existed before him; therefore, he didn't know who he was serving, for the divine takes shape in all. Akbar designed his world by painting a vision in his mind and channelling his energy through visualization toward an ultimate manifestation. All of creation was art and that was Akbar's intoxication of choice; his curiosity and intelligence was reflected in every masterpiece.

A story circulated of how Akbar desired a gold tea set with precious crystals he dreamt of. Dreams were known to be the voice of the subconscious. The tea set was crafted from the finest china, inlaid with the most beautiful golden calligraphy, and bejewelled with sapphires, rubies, and emeralds. He made it his personal mission to find an artist who could create the masterpiece.

It took him three years of sifting through 5560 artisans until he found the one. While on a spiritual journey camel-trekking with his tribesmen, he stumbled upon a remote Turkish village in the desert. Akbar began to question if anyone knew of an artist with the skills to create such a masterpiece. He was directed to a remote dirt hut occupied by a very old man. When Akbar arrived, he was shocked to see a crippled man.

They stared at each other in silence.

Eventually, the old man broke the silence and told him to leave what was needed and no more, and to come back seven days later. Akbar didn't even have a chance to explain what it looked like.

After seven days, Akbar returned to find an empty hut. Bewildered, he sat in the middle of the dirt floor and closed his eyes to meditate, wondering if this was all just an illusion of the earthly plane. He wondered whether the seven days signified a deeper meaning. Many ancient scrolls proclaimed the number "7" as the secret code for the reality hidden under illusions. When he came out of his trance-like state, he saw the crate on which the old man sat had mysteriously reappeared.

Upon it was the tea set.

He ran out of the hut like a wild Arabian in great search of the old man. But he was nowhere to be found. Akbar believed the old man was a "siddhi," one who can assume any form they wish because of paranormal and magical powers acquired through yoga and meditation. Inside the kettle was the quote he saw in his dream and never spoke: "Your mind is the vehicle for growth."

पञ्च

My mother, Plondregi Begum, was the vision of a goddess: an endless black mane that fell to her waist, eyes of such depth that they spoke for her, glimmering golden skin, and a silhouette that hypnotized all. She was reciting Sufi poetry in the gardens when she looked down at her stomach and realized I was ready to arrive. The help immediately took her to her quarters; some laid cold cloths and compresses on her head and feet, while others massaged peppermint on her scalp to relax and soothe her. Fresh rose oil was dripped and massaged onto her forehead to open up her third eye as sweat dripped off her body. Secret tea recipes were administered to alleviate the pain and act as a mild sedative.

My father's name was Abdul Hassan Asaf Khan. He was compassionate and wise with a charming presence; his humor intoxicated everyone. His calm demeanor was due to meditation and living in the moment, as well as the discipline of life which he often spoke. He was tall and lean; dark and exotic, perfectly sculpted. My father was madly in love with my mother. He could never take his eyes off of her. He craved her like a deadly addiction. His energy was playfully intense towards her. He even traipsed in and out of the quarters, singing her the most elaborate ghazals as he awaited my birth. My mother's disapproving reactions and banishment from the quarters spoke otherwise. She sent him off knowing he was deeply loved. Even in challenging moments, she still loved his fancy and flavorful ways.

When he was given permission to enter again, he dashed through the bedroom door. Parwar, my three-year-old sister, accompanied him. She wasn't as excited as him, but deeply curious. He cradled me in his arms and unravelled all the precious jewels he stowed away for me. They shined brighter than the summer sun that came to greet me as I opened my eyes on September 1st, 1593 to become Arjumand Banu Begum.

My mother was understandably exhausted and went to sleep shortly thereafter. Father cradled me to sleep, telling me fables of the desert and how there was once a beggar who became a king, and then died a beggar. No matter how many endless riches and gold the king acquired, he was always a beggar because his spirit was poor. That was the first prophetic message I was told as a child born into nobility. Life has no meaning with earthly riches; they are mortal. Mortality dies; however, that which lives forever, and cannot be bought, is immortal. Everything was precious and born from God's vision.

I learned this while holding on for dear life as we flew in and around the palace on our flying carpets. My favorite pastime was flying through the arched doorways as fast as I could. My father and I would meet in a variety of rooms in the palace and sit upon inscriptions and fly through its tale. Many of his dreams were stitched into the luxurious silk and cashmere carpets; as such, I could fly on them and experience his visions. It was another form of how he expressed what lived within his soul.

I had my very own fine carpet collection, woven with enchanting pharaohs and sphinxes, harvest moons, past and present kings, and exotic cats and spiritual sutras. The fine threads foretold the finely stitched stories imbedded with my secret meanings and messages.

Sometimes, I let the carpet's energy guide me through its visions. Other times, I made up my own tales. I loved to drive my carpet as much as I loved to be taken on a wild ride. My father taught me at a young age when to assume my power and when to relinquish in a silent state.

षट्

The palace was endless, no beginning and no end. I could easily get lost inside if I wasn't careful to map out where I was. Six floors of sprawling, elegant regal craftsmanship were built of red sandstone and luxurious marble. Jali-latticed screens were precisely placed throughout the palace, creating mesmerizing shadows of geometric patterns. The grandiose balconies allowed you to sit at great heights and gaze into the far distance—beyond Agra, India.

Lavish domes and archways linked heaven and earth. Elaborate doorways and turquoise-tiled mosaic entries were complementary introductions into exquisite rooms, highlighting the beautiful white marble within. Some of the sculptures were platinum and named after Hindu deities; others were noble beings and kings—or exotic animals, such as Akbar's prized white cheetah.

The 24-karat gold heirloom mirrors were intricately painted, the commissioned vanity mirrors had faces painted upon them, and the magical mirrors allowed you to walk through visions of prophecies. There were sky-high mirrors that continued from room to room and down the halls— where dreams never ceased to end. Miniscule ones were cut into shapes that could easily be missed. The gardens were magnificent. Indo-Islamic architecture intertwined with flowing fountains, pools, and canals surrounded by blossoming roses, luscious greenery, and statuesque trees.

The palace was imbedded with secret geometric codes and patterns; the number "4" symbolized the perfection of God's unchanging laws. There were tunnels that led to hidden vaults behind the walls, which held ancient sacred texts, potions and tinctures, minerals, alchemy, and secret forecasts and prophecies. The cosmic celestial room had detailed maps with every star that existed and its planetary placements, as well as what transits they were in and how we were affected. Not only were they consulted for astrology, but they held powerful talismans that were consulted for battle.

At the age of six, I conjured Shiva's energy of creation and destruction. My energy was unstoppable, a whirlwind tornado. My father would laugh, swoop me into his arms, and swing me around to change my life's direction. In a playful tone, my mother would either demand I behave or would orchestrate a way for me to run free that didn't command her attention.

I believe my mother began her contractions with me at four in the morning; consequently, this is why I'm always up at this godly hour. I carefully cracked my mother's bedroom door open just a little, making sure I couldn't see my father. She looked so beautiful with her black, flowing tresses draped over her cotton night dress and white sheets.

I slowly tiptoed to her closet. I ran back to the door just to make sure no one was coming. You can never be too safe during one of these high-stakes missions. I walked up to her armoire and turned the key to the right and nervously giggled, and then looked at my mother. It was designed with demi-gods and elephants, camels and tigers; each section told a different story.

The key always made a clanging sound against the elaborate lock. Seeing as how this was my mother's closet, it was perfectly color-coordinated. So much so, that all the hues and shades matched perfectly.

I took a quick breath for inspiration and opened my eyes. A million dazzling little lives were folded and hung on hooks and hangers; some were discreetly hid in drawers.

Who was I?

What did I want to be?

I didn't have much time for such thoughts under these tight restraints. I would have to decide quickly. I closed my eyes and let my hands guide me. That was how I came to choose a ruby-encrusted kurta top, a diamond lehenga skirt, and gold-woven camel jhutis.

This needed to be a perfectly timed mission.

Quickness was of the essence. As I got closer to the door and farther away from her bed, I sped up silently. It was difficult, as I loved to thump and stomp. I readjusted the garments in my delicate little hands as they slipped from my grip. They felt so heavy in between my fingers. I started to hunch over from the weight, like a bandit on the run from a heist. As soon as I reached the door, I looked back and smirked.

I gently closed the door and zipped away.

I ran down the white marble tunnel. It was like a never-ending sari that went around and around. The rich, textured marble floor was cold on my feet, which helped with my brisk pace. I looked around again to make sure no one was there. I ran past the prayer room, which I bowed to, before making a mad dash to the library.

I took the key out of the door before I walked in. I was sure to shut the door and lock it from the inside. To be honest, I'd lost the keys inside before and locked myself in. So, this time, I was sure to see where I put them—right on the peacock table.

It was rather embarrassing to lock myself in a room and then have Teetu climb through a window to let me out, feverishly denying my thievery while being caught red-handed. Teetu worked for our family for as long as I could remember. He told me that I was the reincarnation of Hanuman, the monkey god, because I was always swinging off the railings and peepal trees.

I loved to hide jewels and things, pretending that I didn't know where they were, even though I knew better. It was a little sneaky and mischievous, giving credence to my monkey title.

This was one of my favorite rooms in the palace.

Floor-to-ceiling mural paintings of the Mahabharata, Ramayana, and Persian epics were encapsulated by breathtaking windows, which opened up into the gardens. Countless texts and antiquity novels were left behind, unsigned. Royal furniture was crafted in indulgent rich purples and ruby reds. Beautiful water pipes, writing pens, knives, and swords instigated delightful conversations. There were silver-carved trays with Victorian Mughal tea sets; heavenly fragrances drifted from the gardens and mingled with the incenses that lingered throughout the palace. It was said that Akbar's father had no gifts for his courtiers, so he anointed them with a rose attar and proclaimed that his newborn heir's fame would spread like the decadent sweetness of the rose.

It did.

I needed some time to catch my breath—to unwind a little. So, I put the clothing on the arm of a wooden chair and poured myself a glass of water from a clay jug. I loved to see seeds floating and sugarcane cubes transparently blended in. The palace had me on a sugar limit very early on. As much as I protested, very little was done to change that. It was a treat on special occasions—or when I had the power to sneak what I could from their dishes when they turned their watchful eyes away. I learned early on that one must devise other ways to get what one wants.

I took my kurta pyjamas off slowly. I was still a little sleepy, as I expended a lot of energy already. My waist-long mane was a mess. I managed to escape not getting it re-braided last night by rising before anyone could find me this morning. I cupped my hands and breathed into my palms. A slight smell: a little tart and sour as usual. I hadn't chewed any neem yet. I knew that these teeth would leave soon, so it wasn't a priority to take care of what remained.

As I whipped off my kurta bottoms, I heard the sounds of a tear. *Oh no, not again.* I was famous for tearing and breaking things with my hasty movements. I pulled my pajama pants down and grabbed the ruby top. As soon as I put it on, it fell to the floor; it was now a dress.

I put the diamond skirt over it.

I took my hair out of what was left of its so-called design, flinging the cloth tie across the room like a warrior with a slingshot. I tried to tighten the ruby top by cinching the waist, but that didn't work well. My mother would kill me if I ruined it, so I decided I would keep the top as a dress, as it looked like one anyway.

I grabbed the gold jhutis. My mother's feet were so large next to mine, even though they were quite small and delicate. I decided I would shove my toes to the top to give me a grip and some support. I walked up to the mirror and made a grand turn to face myself.

The sun broke through the windows to greet me. I ran to the window to display my adoration. This also meant my mother would be up now—or very shortly. I peered outside the door to make sure no one was around. If anyone saw me, it would be obvious what I was up to.

It was clear for a perfect exit.

I made a beeline for the marble spiral staircase. The bloody kurta top was so long that it kept catching on my heels as I zoomed up the stairs.

सप्त

I cautiously and slowly pushed the door open and crept along the wall. I could see that my mother's bed was empty and the sheets were unravelled, like ocean waves. This meant that she was already getting a reading done on the balcony overlooking the gardens. I couldn't change without making noise; also, I would be in clear view of her closet.

Why didn't I change downstairs?

I dashed across the room and leapt into the large white armchair on the balcony overlooking the grounds. Boldly, I acted as if nothing was out of place. My mother's eyes hawked me. I knew that she wondered how I got out of my kurta pyjamas and into her kurta without her knowing.

I poured myself a cup of tea. I didn't like it when the help did things for me, nor did I call them servants—*serve-ants*. Well, ants did serve the queen. But I wasn't a queen.

With the cup to my mouth, I watched as Kabir sang Shiva discourses to my mother. When I finally glanced at her with my face still half in the cup, she looked back at me and smirked. I smirked back. I then put the cup down and gave her a smile that covered the entirety of my face as I gracefully crossed my legs.

There would be no me without Kabir.

He was an heirloom in our family, our trusted advisor and the destiny-layer and designer of my life. He predicted my birth and as soon as I was born, he placed me in a pool of water with crystals all around. He walked circles, chanting enchanting texts as I giggled. The water even changed colors from emerald green to violet with his mystical hymns and sutras. I was blessed and protected in an invisible chakra shield from the moment I appeared. We always took his guided advice and those he channelled from the constellations.

Kabir was gifted to my mother when she was a child. When parents bestowed a mystic upon their child, they gave them a spiritual advisor for life. It is extremely difficult to become one, especially for royalty; the exceptional ones are rare.

I loved everything about Kabir, down to his tattered, plain-white kurta pyjamas. His pyjamas showed what he ate that day, and what he ate every day of his ancient existence. His camel flats were two different nude tones and the heel on his right sandal was worn to the floor. The camel hide was coming off. My mother gifted him with many new luxurious garments, even basic staples. But he never wore them. He would tell us how grateful he was; yet, we never saw him in any of the gifts.

He usually kept a snow-white bun that sat lopsided on his head. Sometimes, he tied it in a turban; other times, he left his silver tresses out wild and loose, like my horse Moonlight.

All seers seemed to talk in hypnotic, calm tones—earthy and always grounded. I often wondered if it was because of the potions they inhaled or the secret smokes I saw them ingest. Some had beards; others had Rajasthani moustaches that twirled perfectly up to the sky—like a staircase to heaven. Kabir's moustache curled toward the rooftop of the palace and when he went into a deep meditative state, I would silently twist it to the precise points where I thought the astral messages were coming from. My mother would scold me, more as a formality than anything else. He would open his eyes when the time was right and smile.

I memorized and programmed every word Kabir spoke; anything that floated off of his lips mesmerized me. I knew he was special. Mother would always quote Kabir about the nature of God: "God is the invisible one inside the breath."

He spoke of remedies to heal her minor health ailments: which herb and plant would serve best. Neem for cleansing the blood and parasites; lemons with peppermint for vitality and clarity. Triphala for stomach issues when they arose and the rarest honeys for skin beautification. He spoke of how more riches were to come to the family, though my parents never asked about monetary gains.

Kabir was talking up a storm and staring at the skies as he gathered cosmic messages when all of a sudden, he just stopped. He didn't breathe. He was dead still.

Pure silence, except the earth's echo.

The universe stopped; I felt it.

His intense gaze locked onto me. Suddenly, he grabbed my left hand and started tracing the lines of my palms—in and around, up and down, and to those that were unfinished. He stared into the sky once more and traced the lines of the universe up above and linked the two. He put his hands in prayer position at his chest and sat in silence.

The stars aligned with his thoughts.

"She is blessed."

My mother was quick to respond. "Seemingly so with all that she is, who she is, and what is to come." She left her response open-ended in anticipation of Kabir's response.

Kabir quipped back. "Yes, yes, yes—three times of what is to come." He paused. "What is to come?" he asked the invisible stars.

My mother looked into his eyes.

"A maharaja is to come to the maharani. She is to marry the grandest of all kings in the near and now foretold future. But this is not any king. No, not an ordinary king. He is extraordinary, out of the ordinary. He is the true meaning of what a king is."

I laid down and watched as he traced more invisible lines in the sky, outlining the specific stars that gave him the premonitions. They were hard to see in between the sun and the clouds, but we knew they were there.

"However, there is something that must be done. They must wait five years after their introduction for marriage. Within that time, an engagement will take place. But she must wait. Not before, not after. When she is 19, the cosmic stars will be aligned for their destined union. He is majestic, with the ravishing heart of a tiger—very brave."

I spoke up. "I've always been a tiger. I have patiently waited and asked my mother for my very own for a long time. This brings so many blessings to my ears. To know that one day I shall have one of my very own. I have seen those in costume, but not of character."

"He walks the dirt right now," Kabir continued. With that, he placed his palms to the floor in gratitude. "He will love all things godly—the arts, poetry, philosophy, and nature. Just like you, maharani."

My mother raised her hands up to the skies and smiled in gratitude to the gods.

"He will love her like no other. A temple of love is destined, 'a teardrop on the face of eternity.' Nothing that his eyes have laid sight upon or experienced will be his beloved. This love was born once again from long ago; they are each other's destiny. They will bring the universe to higher realms of cosmic consciousness because of their unconditional love."

Kabir had no understanding of time, unless it was destiny. He spoke of how life had no beginning and no end, for God doesn't have a clock. Time was beyond him and what he knew or could understand in his mystical world, unless it was spoken in the moment. He said a moment was a moment, just like a breath. Within that breath so much life is held and one can change or manifest their destiny in accordance with the depth and connection to the breath. He said that when you don't hold onto anything, then you are in the present; you can then experience the past, future, and present all in the same moment. That was why he was so omnipotent: time didn't exist. When it was gone, it ceased to exist again.

He didn't even know his age or when his birthday was. If anyone asked him, he would say it was today. I figured he did this for the desserts, definitely not for the gifts. He spoke of how everyday is a birthday when God gifts you the presence of life.

He looked at me quizzically. "How old are you now?"

I raised my right hand up to show five fingers, and then two other fingers on my left hand; I scrunched one of my fingers in half to show I was six. "I'm six. I'm six and a half. My birthday is in a few months."

"Since you are almost seven now, well, six and half you say, close to seven years from now you shall encounter each other. But when you meet, remember you are only to marry when you are 19, on May 10th, 1613. For that is your maktub, your written destiny."

My mother was in a hypnotic state when I glanced at her.

Kabir resumed sitting in lotus pose.

After some time, Kabir slowly stood up and bowed to my mother, placing his hands on her feet. She stood up and took his hands in gratitude, gracefully touching his feet and gathering the cosmic forces that spread from his toes.

She followed behind him in silence.

अष्ट

I put my mother's kurta, lehenga skirt, and jhutis back into her closet exactly the way I had found them. Well, my version at least, as she said on numerous occasions.

I felt like doing something…but what?

My eyes took me into a mural of a hundred maharajas sitting at a table eating dinner—every king from every century exchanging thoughts. I saw myself within the painting, advising and conducting legalities and formalities destined only for men. I knew that this was a prophecy of what was to come. I was born a rebel. I wanted to do things that others couldn't or wouldn't dare to dream of. And then it came to me: I would paint this soon-to-be king of mine.

I dashed to my bedroom and watched as Kabir walked through the gardens, past the guards, through the peacocks and monkeys, and ultimately disappearing like a djinn into the shade. It took nearly thirty minutes on foot just to arrive at the palace gates, as the grounds were so vast.

My nose had been caught by the spices of cardmonon, saffron, and bay leaves that lingered through the hallways and up into my bedroom. Lunch would be served soon and that meant my father would be back. I crawled underneath my bed and grabbed my silver-encrusted chest. There were tigers all over it—in addition to a variety of exotic cats, including panthers and cheetahs. I adored this chest. My mother had it commissioned for me when I was born.

I opened the tiger-head latches and found an array of paint blocks and color pigments. I would have to mix and create the colors from dried fruit flowers and plants. I needed to add flour in order to get the desired consistency and texture. I never put the flour away properly, so it was lightly sprinkled over everything in my room. I grabbed my tree-bark and horsehair brush and began to imagine.

How is love created?

Where did love come from?

What did love feel like?

How is love described?

Would I love this little maharaja?

I set up my chair and bark canvas underneath the dome that led from my bedroom. I looked at the grounds for inspiration; the natural light would be my guide and muse. Perhaps I could stare into the sky like Kabir did and wait for a prophetic picture to appear.

It didn't.

I squeezed my eyes shut and figured the harder I squeezed, the greater the vision of the king. At six and a half, that was how I believed things came true.

It didn't.

I walked around the bed in circles, thinking that the ritual would draw him near.

It didn't.

I made a mad dash and jumped onto my bed. I sat in lotus pose and stared at the ceiling. Staring at the ceiling would be like looking at an empty canvas upon which I could create.

It failed to help.

I then decided it didn't matter if it was an elephant's head on a lion's body or a falcon's face on a human body. I started to draw an outline and added colors along the way. Details of a nose emerged with dark mysterious eyes and a thick, wavy black mane like a lion's—like mine. It slowly turned into a vision of a little boy who was a few years older than me. He wore jodhpurs and a kurta tunic as he sat on a black stallion— —a little maharaja. In the background, there was an owl. I added that because I wanted a Bengal eagle owl.

I stared deep into his eyes, allowing him to take me away through the painting. The exact words he spoke to me were: "We are destined for this love." He was very charming and wise. His words became clearer: "I love you and you must love me back."

A knock at the door startled me out of my daydream. Well, it wasn't a dream; I was awake. I looked at the door, knowing the message.

"I'm coming," I responded quickly.

Lunch was to be held in the lavish Turkish formal dining room. My toes sank into the luxurious Persian carpets as I found my seating. The beautifully carved ornate lanterns and painted plates perfected the exotic ambience. No extra placements and seats meant no guests or visitors would join us—just my father, my mother, Parwar, and me.

They were already seated.

I had a habit of showing up late. Even when I was on time, I was told I was late. I told them their sundials were off. Mine was correct, as I collected directly from the sun and not from the instruments that sat in their pockets.

The table was covered in vegetables and curries. The flavors and aromas, along with the spices, drenched the room in a mesmerizing fragrance, a heavenly aromatic musical.

Food has always taken me away. My parents taught me at a young age how food is medicinal and nutrients are needed for vitality and healing. We ate an ayurvedic diet, meaning we ate for our soul's consciousness. The food selection depended on seasons and the moon's phases. Everything was complementary, interdependent yet intertwined. I liked to see which dish was the most dominant and how many other dishes it could overtake. Some had no aroma, but the dish itself was mouth-watering and divine.

There was help in all four corners of the room: north to serve, east to take dishes, west to pour, and south to attend to any other requests. My mother loved to eat leisurely; whereas, my father loved to devour. Parwar liked to pick at her food and I ate depending on my feelings. That also dictated my pace and how I ate. Today, I decided I would have a little bit of everything. I wanted a full plate because I missed breakfast and worked up quite the appetite.

I liked food served to me. Whenever I tried to pour something, it spilled outside of the plate and stained everything.

I was famous for trails.

Even though Parwar was only a couple of years older than me, she was more refined. My mother advised me to watch her; to be honest, there wasn't much to watch. Parwar was beyond boring. It seemed as if she wasn't enjoying herself or her food. She was so careful and precise that it seemed as if she was a puppet on a string. Pulled here, pulled there: everything was orchestrated, ruling her every gesture. Maybe that's why we didn't play or talk much. She was structured, whereas I had no rules.

"Arjumand, what did you get up to today?"

Silence.

"Any type of trouble?" my father asked.

I could feel my mother's eyes lock upon me as my father's questions flowed one after another. I responded while staring into my plate. "Oh, not much. How about you, Shah?" I loved to call my father *king*, even though he wasn't technically a king. Other times, I would call him Maharaja, Raja, or Rai. It also helped to distract from the current issues at hand.

"There hasn't been much on the itinerary, Arjumand. I went to deal with some land of ours and to look into some new horses," my father replied. "I had a discussion with Akbar regarding some acquisitions. And you? Again, I ask, my princess."

I tried to play it off as if there was nothing.

"Oh, you know me—not much. Well, I painted and played, and that is all I can say. That is truly all I can remember."

"Played?" My mother's pitch rose. "What kind of playing?"

"Oh, you know how I am and how it always goes." I twisted my hands so as not to reveal my lack of credibility. I hoped that one of these hand mudras would distract accordingly—that the gods would intercept and save me. I picked this habit up from my mother; it was always a dead giveaway.

Why did I do it now? I would never know.

"Entertain me as always you always do, Princess Arjumand. How did you play?"

"Well, today I painted in my quarters and danced with the peacocks," I replied.

"Does this playing mean you dressed up also?" my mother interrupted.

"Well, to be honest, yes, mother—a little bit. You know, when I woke up this morning, I thought I would pretend not to be me. It's quite boring at times to wake up and be the same person. Do the Shah and Shahbanu not get bored of always being king and queen?" I stared into their eyes, hoping my flattery wooed them. "I must proclaim that I am guilty. I wanted to be you." I cracked a smirk, knowing my mother secretly loved our banter.

"What a wild tiger I have. Highly amusing," my father mused. "Dangerous, too. And how is Parwar, my child?"

"Father, I am as I always am, the same."

"Did you dress up with your sister?" he queried.

"No, father, I looked for her when I got up, but as usual she was nowhere to be found. I had a very busy morning." Parwar continued. "I played in the gardens by myself."

I created pictures in my food. I was more into abstract art today. I had to be discreet in my unrefined mannerisms. Out of the corner of my eye, I saw that the desserts were imminent.

Oh, how I loved sweets.

My father liked it when I allowed my meal to settle. I had slight digestive ailments due to my sensitive stomach and nervous Virgo ways—perhaps because of my highly sensitive nature, too. My father hoped I wouldn't eat so much if I waited, but it just made more room in my stomach.

I anxiously tapped my spoon on the leg of the table, waiting for when I could dive in and attack my heavenly craving. As soon as my mother went in for a bite, I could proceed.

Time continued to tick away.

Oh gosh, she wanted chai. Okay, she was lifting her spoon. I lifted my spoon and jumped into the bowl of liquid sugar and coconut. It slowly dripped down the freeway of my throat and reached the dead-end tunnel of my stomach. The most perfect coconut Gulab jamun: I could feel the sugar rising. I think this is why my father limited me.

"Tomorrow, I have decided that you both will try yoga," my father announced.

"Yoga? What's yoga?" I asked.

"It's a meditation process that will guide you by breath to find self-mastery."

I looked at my mother, wondering if this was part of my preparation to make me a queen—or if she would join. I often saw her practicing in the gardens. I put my hands before me in prayer and closed my eyes to mimic all the gurus I saw.

"Yes, you and your sister will learn what it is like to live inside your body."

"But I thought we did that already?" I asked, still sitting in my godly posture.

"For now, you do," he replied. "You are still children, and the mind has not become your master yet. But there will come a time when you will want to escape and you may become a servant to the mind. And for that you will need discipline. Many experiences will come to you in life as you grow. One needs a great deal of self-compassion and patience of the evolving, changing self."

"Will you join?" I asked.

"I shall if your mother and I finish in a timely manner. This won't be your only time. I know your fondness and appreciation for it will grow," he affirmed. "So, the short answer is—yes."

"And where will this take place?" my sister asked.

"In the gardens tomorrow," he replied.

"In the *garrrrrdens* tomorrow," I belted. The dishes shook from my voice. This was what I meant about the sugar kicking in.

The dishes were being walked out, denying me more.

I thanked Teetu and all of the help. I always felt grateful and lucky for what I was blessed with; my parents instilled that in me since my first breath. My father raised his right hand in the air, palm facing up. This meant that my sister and I were allowed to dismiss ourselves from the table. I kissed my mother and father on the cheek, and then ran to the kitchen to talk to Teetu.

Teetu always knew when I consumed too much sweetness because I zipped in and around the kitchen, disturbing him and all the staff.

"Teetu, guess what?" I asked.

"Guess what, princess? What is it you wish to tell me?"

I hopped onto the table, which was framed by fresh-cut fruits and vegetables. "There is something you should know. I have to tell you something. It's a secret, but I shall tell you. Since I do not share with just anyone, know that I am telling you and only you. Okay, here it is."

I pulled out a long blank scroll and read from it. I made up my thoughts along the way. I cleared my throat as my father did when speaking about aristocratic matters. "To whom it shall concern," I whispered. "Arjumand is going to marry a king. So, now instead of being nobility, she will be a queen."

"A queen you will be." Teetu then bowed.

I called him in closer by directing him with my finger. "But Teetu, even if I'm a queen, you have to promise me one thing."

"Well, princess, I can't promise unless I know."

"You can promise without knowing," I pleaded. "Agree to the request: *I promise to do as Arjumand says.* Teetu, you must come with me. If I am ever to leave this palace for another, you must come. If we are to stay, you stay; but if I am to move, you must move, too."

"Oh, but what about your parents?" Teetu reasoned. "What if they need me?"

"Oh, Teetu, I need you more. Believe me."

Teetu taught me so much: how to get my monkey to jump on my back; how to get Looki, my cat, to dance and listen to my commands; how to read magical scriptures and manifest ideas through my heart; and personal recipes for all my whims and fancies in life.

The list was without end.

I hopped off the table and wrapped my arms around his waist. I ran out of the kitchen and yelled down the hall, "Trust me, you can't live without me. What will you do without me? I just know that we can never be apart."

"What would I do without you, princess? You're right," he admitted. I could hear his faint laughter echoing down the hallway even though I was at the palace's entrance.

नव

I made sure to check that the guards were doing their jobs throughout the gardens. All was in order. There were 40 in total, in all corners, locations, and towers. We had far more, but they were only needed in the event of an attack or when my father felt he required them.

I decided to stroll through the enchanting clay labyrinth. The ancient worlds said that labyrinths were the escape of samsara (cyclicity of life) and karma. It was also known that they conducted magic and kept hostile energies at bay. There was always something there to provide random entertainment. It was four floors, faced the east, and boasted over 500 different entries. The trick was to walk the correct path so that the seven routes led you to the fulfillment of your wishes.

I decided to try the starred-door entry and saw my white rabbit, Kashmir, testing his fate; he didn't care much for my ways, so he disappeared. Shortly after, Parwar decided to do the same thing and joined me. "Can you hear me, Arjumand? I'm here."

I felt her timid toes and then heard her voice when I placed my ear against the wall. It was known since ancient times that servants communicated and devised plans of deceit against their masters by such a technique.

I invited her for one of our infamous games of chess. Well, more like moving royal headpieces. A beautiful grass chess set was inlaid with Turkish marble and boasted exquisite crystal chessmen.

My father had them specially commissioned.

There were all of India's great rulers painted with such precision and perfection that even Akbar agreed to the identical resemblance. Some of the figurines were crafted in regal poses with their hands in their laps. This made it very easy for me to sit on their hands and ask my opponent to slide me to my desired position. It was easy to slide the pieces on the glossy surface of the marble, as the floor was always quite slippery; and after a monsoon, I could really go flying, holding on for dear life.

After some time pretending to be kings and queens, we followed the hypnotizing hymns, which lead us to Majid's ghazals. He sat on a golden crescent-moon rug spun of the finest zari threads. It was specifically created for his sacred chanting. My father thought that vibrations and good omens would keep Allah—and all of the gods and goddesses up above—joyful. The way he played the sitar and created such magnificence with a single chord was otherworldly; animals would gather and sing along. He channeled the universally divine—none were to be left out or to be forgotten.

Majid always kept his eyes closed, like he was intoxicated by the gods' responses to his offerings. He would sway ever so slightly, like a cobra being charmed.

None of his creations were planned.

As he said, "Does God plan what to do next?"

He always faced the same direction—southeast. The Hindu symbolic meaning of southeast is for receiving; this cosmic alignment was channeled since the beginning of time. We received what the gods gave and gave back, for our hands were created from theirs.

As dusk settled, the clouds descended and the sun fell behind the walls of Agra. Teetu brought me a tray of yellow lentil dhal and goat yogurt for dinner, and lychee and mango salad for dessert.

"Your parents have gone for dinner, so you and your sister have some time. But soon, you must go to sleep."

As he walked away, I kept my eyes on him as I nibbled on my rabbit snacks. He seemed so much larger than life, so much more than his minuscule frame. He was short with the thickest eyelashes and hair. His dark cocoa complexion complemented all of his other features, especially his hair. He usually kept it tied back when he worked; other times, it was wrapped in a sloppy turban.

I watched the tales of the sky unfold. I saw that the stars were speaking to the canvas of the sky. I always wondered if my father was a dealer for the galaxy, as many stars were adorned on my mother's body—her neck, her fingers, her hair, and even her clothing.

My eyes fought a tremendous battle with my heavy eyelids in order to gaze at the stars even longer. I heard Parwar speak of how she was heading for bed. Meera's soles clinked against the marble floor until they were next to me.

"You know what time it is? I know you can hear me, little one," she teased.

My grandparents found Meera as a little girl on the side of the road selling vegetables. They asked her if she wanted to live with them and work for them, which she did until their final breaths. My mother told her many times just to live with us and to stop working. At her age, she didn't need to do anything for us—just be with us, so that we could take care of her. After all, she was family. But she said she liked to keep busy. I think it was because she never experienced anything else.

I kept my eyes closed, hoping she would think I was asleep and would let me sleep among the stars. When I tried to play "sleep," it was very easy to detect; my expressions told all. I could see her fingers inching and creeping near, going for my tummy. Then she stopped and looked up at the stars. Her fingers remained frozen in the air. I don't know what took her away—what mesmerized her.

She laid down next to me and stargazed. After some time, lying cuddled side by side, I could feel as she drifted off into a blissful, deep sleep. Shortly after, I, too, fell asleep. We were to dream amongst the constellations as gods, far away from the mortal world.

दश

I awoke to the melodic chirpings of crickets and cuckoo birds. When I opened my raven eyes, all I could see was a sky full of feathers. There were camouflaged falcons and white owls alongside rainbow parrots and indigo pigeons—and everything else in between. It was a painter's palette of perfection.

I rolled to my right and saw that the blanket was bare; however, it still held the shape of Meera's body. I must have slept in, as I could hear the voices of those who already began their daily work on the grounds.

Today was the day that Parwar and I were to take up yoga. I dashed downstairs to the gardens, and there he was. I looked at him, wondering how this man who looked like a character out of an enchanted tale, with his purple turban and yellow genie pants, was going to teach us yoga. His turban was elaborate and shiny; the type one wore to a wedding, not to teach a yoga class in the gardens.

Where did my father find such characters?

He looked like a single breath could knock him over.

"Hello, girls," he sang.

"Hello, master," I sang back.

"Yoga, yoga, yoga, and here we are. I am Rakesh. Your parents must have told you about me. I am here for yoga." With that, he tumbled into a handstand with one hand, and then proceeded to throw both of his legs over his head. So much for Rakesh being fragile. He started tapping his body and telling us he was opening his chakras, and then he tapped in between his eyes, informing us he was awakening his third eye and to keep watch.

"Girls, girls, the eye is open," Rakesh announced. "Join in, girls. Open up those colors; open up the *eye*, the *I*."

I poked my sister.

"Open up that other eye you have." I giggled.

She wasn't amused. Parwar looked at him as if he escaped from the jungle. She barely let her fingertip touch her third eye. I fell in love with Rakesh; he had such a zest for life. Not to mention I was in awe and baffled by the contortions and shapes that his slender body could create.

"Okay, let's start in tree pose."

"You want us to become trees?" my sister asked.

"But before you become a tree let me tell you the magical story of how vriksasana (tree pose) began, for all poses in yoga come from a deep meaning that channel the gods." He continued. "When the demon King Ravana captured Queen Sita, he took her to Lanka and presumed that she would fall madly in love with him—or at least with one of his ten beautiful faces. His riches and power hypnotized all, but Sita saw nothing. She said, 'I am your prisoner, not your guest, and I will never be your queen. Rama is my beloved and when he finds you, you will wish your evilness had no existence.' The demon god replied by saying that he was a kind man and that she had one year to accept her fate as being his or she would be killed."

His story continued. "Ravana's servants were ordered to watch over her. They were hideous creatures with the faces of goats, dogs, and other animals and had innumerable eyes and body parts with coarse hair that randomly grew. They were given the task to speak negativity in Sita's ear to break her faith of Rama's return so she would bow down before Ravana. Sita's only friend was an Ashoka tree, 'without sorrow,' that lived outside the palace walls. The Ashoka tree was known to be a healer and held infinitesimal powers. Being the daughter of Bhumi Devi (Mother Earth), Sita knew that she had to connect within and sat beneath the tree of sorrow, asking its deep roots to connect her to the divine and back to Rama. From dusk to dawn, through every breath and thought, she recited 'Rama, Rama, Rama' with faith that the universe would hear her words. The universe was conjuring its own plan of saving Sita, with Rama summoning Hanuman as a messenger to take a gold ring inscribed with the words 'Rama, Rama, Rama' to present to Sita. As Sita sat beneath the tree of wisdom, Hanuman, the monkey god, flew in and spoke her lover's name. He presented her with the talisman gold ring. With that, her heart spoke and she knew."

I moved into tree pose after watching his example. My leg positioned in the number-four stance. I even added a little back bend.

"Wow, very, very good. Your mind must be just as flexible," he said. "An open mind comes with an open body. Let me quote the Bhagavad Gita: 'Man is made by his belief; as he believes, so he is.' If you are not your beliefs or your limitations, then I ask, what are you when you can become everything?"

I had a great many prophetic visions of what my life was going to be like. I played with visions in my head, watching what thoughts came and went and I allowed for them to manifest in my universe. I could breathe in ways I never before experienced and move to forms that delighted and astonished me. I could feel undiscovered thoughts and emotions through breath and by way of pose.

I requested to see Rakesh every day.

He always had new teachings and themes; as such, I never got bored. Sometimes, we practiced in the maze in animal costumes, which I suggested. Parwar would join in when she felt like it, which was very rare.

Mughal women of great status were expected to be highly cultured and informed in every regard. I became engrossed in literature and the arts. Who didn't like an entertaining woman with thought-provoking ideas?

I counted down the days, awaiting the arrival of the king by drawing one star for every day that passed, which drew us closer to meeting. I reasoned that I could erase some of the stars if it took longer than Kabir predicted or cut a few in half.

My mother questioned why I suddenly had a ceiling of stars. I announced that it was part of my new painting exhibit and if I wasn't allowed to sleep among the real stars, I could at least create my own galaxy in my bedroom. The stars I painted were all unique. Some I filled with sparkles, which were leftover shavings from diamonds that my father gave me; others were created with 24-karat gold. And some were painted with the most elaborate mosaic designs.

On this very night, I gazed upon the stars as I did yoga on my balcony, chanting to the moon. I asked the gods in the sky what the universe was—what our purpose was. All of a sudden, the moon changed into the number one from a crescent moon. All of the stars joyfully danced around the moon as the moon suddenly shone a light right through me. I thought the moon was going to take me, right then and there, and put me into the sky and make me a star. It splattered into a white light that sprayed out like a spectrum of lightning bolts.

I ran downstairs to ask my father if he saw such a sight, but since he hadn't, his only explanation was that it was monsoon season and the rains and heat made the gods feisty. When I went back the next morning, there was a stone shaped in the number one on the floor covered in the white light that consumed me.

That was when I decided, if we are all one, I will face my fear and ride our untameable black Arabian, Moksha. I hinted to my father that I wanted the most complicated and moody stallion of all. Perhaps I would be needed in battle one day.

"Arjumand, marriage is so far away and I doubt this king you speak of will allow for such behavior and conduct. Not only that, women don't go to battle—only men do. And a stallion? Why ever would you want to start on a horse that has the same temperament as you? Unpredictable." My father started to chuckle. "Oh Allah, two of her—imagine."

He raised his hands to the skies and laughed.

"I don't find this to be such a humorous proposition, father. I am serious. Are you listening? I have requested very little in the palace. I do not ask for things like Parwar does. But this? Well, this is something I must learn. What if the palace is invaded and I must help? What if that is the only way to escape? Should I not know how to ride the fiercest spirit? Is that not what life is? Riding the fiercest spirit within?"

He remained silent, organizing his mind as logically as he could to this illogical, daring request. He shook his head. "My dearest Arjumand, the problem is that you make far too much sense and I just cannot say *no* to this face of yours. It's true. You ask for almost nothing, except for the impossible—which you say is nothing. If your mother was to find out, she would have my head." He scratched his turban. "Okay, meet me outside by the stalls later today. Your mother has a chai party. All of the ladies are coming up with new chai recipes. They say cinnamon chai, lemon chai, ginger chai, black chai. Chai…chai, chai, chai." He sang all the way down the corridor.

I had to make sure I executed my plan properly and precisely, and that Parwar wasn't around. Who better to question than Teetu? He knew where everyone was, even if they were spirits in invisible places. Ghosts and spirits were welcomed, as they were highly regarded and known for their supernatural powers. They weren't to fear; instead, they were an invitation from the unknown, from those who once lived and now invisibly guided us.

Teetu told me that my grandparents still lived in the palace; and since I never met them in the flesh, he would take me to the tunnels below and ask them to come out. It was actually quite comical when Teetu dressed up as my grandmother. He became her in every sense—even her high-pitched voice and her dramatic hand gestures. He even pretended he was chasing my grandfather with a shoe, which she did when she scolded him. I loved how Teetu was so playful and expressed things that he never got to experience. He only knew what family was like through us.

"Psssssss, psssssss, Teetu."

He turned around.

"What is this snake you are being—psssssss, psssssss?"

He started slinking his body and moving in the air like a cobra. He was so skinny and bony that he actually looked like one. His darker complexion, small face, and enormous eyes didn't help.

"Teetu, I have a question."

"Yeeesssss, Princess."

He slid his tongue out like a snake on the prowl.

"What time is the tea party today? And where?"

"The tea party is at the fifteenth hour and the set-up, well, the set-up…." He scratched his head. "It is on the second level, looking over the fountain today."

"Puuuurrr-fect. Keep it there please."

"Why, Princess?" he asked. "What are you up to? No trouble as such, right?"

"Oh, nothing, nothing, and more nothing."

"I know your nothing, nothing, and more nothing."

I raised my eyebrows and skipped away.

I found my father in the library.

"Father, all is clear: I will see you at the fifteenth hour. She will have no clue; I have made sure of it. I have already made all the necessary arrangements and it is clear to proceed."

"How you get me into these types of situations, Arjumand, I will never know. Are you sure the gods didn't make a mistake and you were supposed to be a boy?"

"Yes, father, I'm the boy you always wanted and the girl you always wanted as well—wrapped up in one. Aren't you lucky you have a demi-god? I shall see you there, father."

I took a few pieces of tree bark so I could dip it in ink and address my first letter to my unknown king.

Dear Maharaja,

I don't know what to call you or who you are....

We have not met, in person or passing, but I have heard many beautiful things about you. I am supposed to be your queen, for it was prophesized by our seer, Kabir. I know many women do not go into battle, nor do they ride, but I am not many women, nor am I like anyone else. I am me, and that is what you shall see.

So, today at the fifteenth hour, when the sun is at its most yellow peak, I shall train with my father on Moksha. Fear not, I will be a better rider than you. I'm sure there are many things we will teach one another. I will inform you of how it goes.

Until then, Inshallah, God willing, I live. Well then, again, God always does everything as I please and is always very willing.

Signing off,

Arjumand

I sealed the envelope and dated it.

Even though my mother would be hastily running around, I needed to be incognito. So, I put together an androgynous ensemble of jodhpurs and a long, loose tunic. Wrapping my mane into a bun, I hid it in a boy's turban. I put my riding boots on and descended the stairs with great caution.

I could see my mother in the distance greeting her guests. It was clear to walk to the stables. I heard Looki right behind me meowing. I swooped her up into my arms and kissed her.

"Looki, you want to ride a horse?"

She purred and snuggled under my neck. I put her down and kissed Ganesh, my elephant, on the trunk before turning the corner to the stables. We had a beautiful selection of rare and exclusive horses of all breeds, shapes, colors, sizes, and ages. My father made sure that they were all tended to. I acknowledged and kissed each one of them on the nose—all sixteen—and then I stood in front of Moksha. I approached him last. He would only allow me to pet him if he so wished. I guess that was what you did when you were an unpredictable black stallion.

Our white Arabian, Moonlight, was the opposite.

She was light, airy, and just wanted to please.

Moksha wanted you to please him. I guess his Sanskrit name was well-suited: liberation from life and death. And with true freedom of self, you do as you please. I will never know why I chose to ride him, maybe because I always played with life and death. Names with the letter "M" were known to be mysterious, but also lucky.

My father told me that nobody could ride or tame Moksha. King Farak, a family acquaintance, planned to set him free into the desert, but my father wouldn't have it. He said he would take him, even if he was never to be ridden. Moksha loved to bask in the sun and roll around in the dirt. Since he was confined for so many years due to his wild ways, he was robbed from the things he loved the most. His face was adorned with a beautiful crystal face-mask, which held India's most precious stones and gems, to keep the flies away. The velvet blankets he wore to bed in the winter had golden tigers stitched with zari threading and the silk pieces were intricately detailed with block printing. I told my father that he must love Moksha more than me, as it seemed he owned more jewels.

Sunjay, who ran the stables, tended to all the animals and trained them. He even slept with them. My parents offered him a room inside, but he said he was where he wished to be.

I turned to see that my father arrived. As he talked to Sunjay, he eyed me and silently questioned my choice of attire. They both looked at me in disbelief. I walked up to them and lowered my voice, introducing myself as Kalki, the avatar of Lord Vishnu, carrier of the horse chariots. "I am here to teach you how to fly on horses," I declared.

My father laughed loudly.

"Oh, you will fly alright—on Moksha." With that, he snapped his fingers. Moksha jumped up on his hind legs and started bucking.

Oh God, I thought. *Okay, wow, I have gotten myself into a rather wild storm.* However, I kept my composure. I learned this in yoga. If I am not balanced and focused within, what I reflect will not be centered.

Sunjay geared Moksha and walked him out to the ring.

My father, Looki, and I followed behind.

"Oh, Looki," I whispered. "We have really done it this time, haven't we?"

Sunjay rode Moksha around the rink a few times. He made it seem so effortless. Then again, he slept beside him nearly every night. My father only got a chance here and there to ride him, and always with Sunjay by his side.

"Are you sure you want to start on God's most fickle, unpredictable temperament? If something should happen to you, my God, your mother…you know. Actually, I don't even know," my father admitted. "I shouldn't even be doing this, Arjumand."

He leaned over the rail, assessing and second-guessing his thoughts. I thought perhaps even Looki believed I'd lost it; she rolled her eyes at me as if to answer.

Sunjay got off and walked over to me. "Ready?"

"Yes, more than ever."

"Okay, come in."

Sunjay explained how to walk around the ring in circles with Moksha side by side—never behind, never ahead. I was to watch Moksha's breath, as that revealed what he wished to do.

That was my first day of instruction.

I hid a few carrots in my pockets. I pulled out my special offering of the three orange gifts and presented them to Moksha.

"You were great, Arjumand," my father declared. "Many do not even get to be in a ring with Moksha. It took me forever. I am not as quick of a learner as you. Day by day, if you keep this up, soon you shall be able to ride on your own."

I unravelled my turban and held it in my hands to smell it. This was the true blood, sweat, and tears that would make me a spiritual warrior.

"Thank you, Sunjay."

"You're most welcome, Arjumand," Sunjay replied.

My father and I held hands as we walked back. I loved how his hands felt, and how they were twice the size of mine. His wisdom and the lines on his hands spoke of his destiny—and it held me in there, somewhere.

My hands outlined the same.

We snuck a decadent dessert together before dinner: coconut ice cream and mangos. It was a good thing we finished when we did, as my mother moved from the second floor to the garden grounds. I saw dishes of all sorts—goodies and fillings, linens and placements of the finest finery, and teapots galore. It was most definitely a chai party if my mother hosted it. There must have been at least a dozen women. They all looked like queens and princesses, even though few were.

एकादशन्

Every day after, my father and I met at the same time for my lessons. And every time I wrote the king a letter to describe my many experiences and what I learned or what challenge I faced. I would always address him in a variety of ever-changing manners: To My Beloved; To the Maharaja; To Whom It May Concern; If you get this letter it means you're someone special. The box grew quite full. Actually, it overflowed. I wrote down of all my feelings and everything I experienced. I wanted him to know everything about my world.

I stayed up one night awaiting an auspicious moon that I knew would change my fate. I channeled Chandra, the moon, relentlessly through mantras I recited, "Om Shraam Shreem Shraum Sah: Chandray Namah." I asked the god of the night who drove the moon chariot across the sky with ten white horses for his white light as guidance.

I slowly opened my bedroom door; it had a habit of creaking at the worst possible times, like when I overtook my mother's closet. I looked left, and then I looked right. I looked both ways once more to be certain—all was clear.

I would have to be on alert, as the guards were vigilant and tuned into everything. I sprinted down the never-ending spiralling stairs. I hid myself against the walls to make sure the guards weren't near. The palace was difficult to maneuver in the dark. It was blacker than black. I could have taken a candle, but seeing how clumsy I was, I probably would have dropped it.

I could rely on my senses: Sounds, smells, what I could feel, and the cracks of light that appeared as guidance from Chandra, the moon, through the windows and open enclosures. Pigeons pecked, so I knew I was near the fountain at the front entrance. I was far enough that I couldn't smell the decadent aromas of Teetu's breakfast preparation. I took a deep breath, which felt rather shallow due to my angst, and I followed the light from the opening of the ceiling to the double doors.

I slowly reached for the steel knob. It was as cold as ice. My hand barely covered half of it, so I had to put one on top of the other. I was having a rather difficult time opening it. Truth be told, I was used to it being opened for me.

"Okay," I spoke to the door. "I have a request. It seems as though I cannot open you. I do have an important meeting at the stables. So, may I ask, would you mind opening yourself for me?"

Attempting again, I put my scrawny little hands on the knob. Like magic, the door blew open. It was as if someone behind me pushed it. I looked around. *Maybe it was the ghost of my grandmother*, I thought, *like Teetu says*. A gust of wind pushed me and I sprinted like Akbar's prized wild white cheetah.

I ran to the stalls like I never had before.

Since it was summer, the horses slept in the open stalls so they could handle the unbearable heat; the wind could breeze through on all sides. It was easy to find Moksha, as he was always alone. He couldn't be with others, except for Moonlight—and even that was dependent upon his moods. I stood before his stall and he slowly walked up to me. He bowed down and I kissed him on his nose. Maybe he only allowed me to do so because he smelled my offering, an apple. I thought this was a good way to break the barrier, a gift and a conversation; this way, he could understand my intent.

"Moksha, you know me well by now. I must say that I am lucky that you have allowed me to be in your presence, given your unpredictable mood swings and your dislike of many people—except for me. But I have a request."

I presented the shiny, crisp crimson apple and he eyed it for a second. He took it as soon as I placed my open palm before him, chomping away. Juices streamed down his mouth and within a few seconds, he was finished.

He just stared at me.

"I'm sorry. One was hard enough to bring." I looked up to the moon to summon her powers. "I'm sorry. There isn't much time, so I must ask my request. Will you let me ride you?"

With that he showed me his power and strength by stretching at full capacity on his hind legs. I didn't know how to take such behavior. Was this his retaliation for not being gifted more apples? Or did Chandra's energy take him away?

I let him settle down for a few minutes.

When he was finished and stood calm, I knew that the time was right. I put his reins on and led him outside. Moksha was never ridden so late, nor had he seen a moon that resembled him in so many ways.

"This is the beginning and the end," I whispered in Moksha's ear. "That's what you are and what we will become——liberation."

He started to walk. Hoof by hoof, he sank deeper into the dirt as he started to pick up his pace. I centered my body and grabbed onto his mane, as this was a sign that he would start to canter.

I had to hold back my screams of delight, for I didn't want to wake anyone or spook Moksha. The moon followed us all around the palace like a dance. I went wherever Moksha desired—through the gardens, around the labyrinth, and over the chess set. We did this for quite some time, never alerting the guards.

I kissed him in between his midnight eyes on his third eye. "You're my first kiss, if you want to know. The next is the king, but I will tell him the truth: that I have kissed another. I will tell him who you were and how amazing this was."

As I opened the screen door, there he was—leaning against it, smiling at me as he drank his chai. "Chai, princess? What were you doing?"

"What was I doing? Well, Teetu, what was I doing? What was I doing?" I looked for the words to appear out of the crisp, thin air.

"Let me take three guesses, princess." He held up three fingers and slurped a sip. "You were looking for Looki, you were bored and up to mischief, or you mastered how to ride Moksha and rode all around the palace like a wild gypsy."

"Well, I found Looki and I'm always up to mischief. Teetu, if you saw what you saw, if you really saw it, then you saw it."

"All these riddles and rhymes: Princess is a great storyteller."

With that, I poured myself a cup of chai and went to write the letter I had long waited to write to the king—telling him how brave I was and how I conquered a fear.

The following day, I showed Sunjay and my father the ease with which I rode Moksha. They were amazed and bewildered by my mastery. My father telling my mother to allow me to do so was another ordeal. She didn't understand why I would want to, how I did so, or the simple fact that I was a girl and it was dangerous. However, my father always found a way.

द्वादशन्

My 10th birthday, my first decade of life. The palace grounds were to be turned into a wild jungle. Family, friends, royalty, and those who desired to attend were to be invited. Looki requested to be dressed up as a peacock, so I placed Vishnu's feathers upon her; she was a rather peculiar peacock. I was a panther, straight from the jungle; my mother and father were the heirs of the jungle, a lion and lioness. Parwar was a dove, Teetu was a monkey, and Meera was a rather odd camel. I wasn't overly fond of celebrations or birthdays, as I was raised to believe that every day was a blessing and my birthday. There were over a thousand guests lingering around. It was fascinating to see characters in costumes conversing and eating.

"My child." My father's voice cracked as he tried to contain his emotions. "I remember waiting for your birth and your mother kicking me out of the quarters when I dressed up in costume and sang to you." My mother made a joke I couldn't hear, but the others were charmed by it. "Oh, how I waited. I just knew we would be blessed, as we already had Parwar and she was sent from the heavens."

Kabir kissed Parwar's cheek.

My father continued. "I designed and created many things for you, as I knew you were born from the gods and stars. I have waited a long time, not knowing when I would gift you this. And then Kabir came to me a few weeks before and as I told him it was your birthday, he said that now would be the time."

I leapt into my father's arms and hugged him. When I detached myself from him, I saw that the imprints of my cat tears stained his lion costume. The yellow fur was darkened in areas of sadness and joy. I didn't want to open the jewelled box in front of everyone, so I put it in my panther pocket.

Moments like this were sacred.

The tablas and sitars started once again. I started to dance and move my body, playing with the energy in the air. My mother gave me a bite of a coconut pastry as I danced with Parwar, the dove.

I had to make a discreet exit, as I wanted to slip away from the party. I grabbed a few tasty treats for my different friends: carrots for Moksha; lentils and fresh vegetables that Looki adored, which were shaped like her face; and Ganesh had her bamboo that Sunjay left nearby.

"Romantic time, is it, Looki? Did you find any suitors?" She looked at me and stared in disgust. The whole time I had her, she never had an interest in any eligible suitors. Many times, I asked if she wanted a companion or needed help in finding a respectful candidate from her numerous offers. I dug into my pocket, but before I could show her what I had, she detected them with a single whiff. She started to purr, rubbing herself and her peacock feathers against my leg, glaring into my eyes.

I crouched down and she inhaled them in one bite.

The sunset became a vast array of purples that melted into a rose-pink essence. I couldn't help but thank the gods for gifting me with such a treasure—my life. I saw Ganesh out of the corner of my eye walking around the grounds. As soon as she saw me, she lifted her trunk to say hello. I made the same gesture back with my panther hands, pretending that I, too, had a trunk.

My father allowed for the animals to roam freely, as he wanted them to be in their natural habitat and in tune with their instincts as much as possible. Never caged or confined, for my father always said, "Imagine if that was you: Would you desire to be the face behind the cage?" Most didn't keep such exotic pets in palaces, nor were they bedazzled in diamond collars or free to roam.

I asked Ganesh to lower her trunk and she slid it to the ground. I walked up it like a ladder and grabbed onto the back of her ears for support. I then crawled onto her back and positioned myself for a ride. Being so high up, near the sky, gave me a sense of majesty. I even did a few yoga poses while we strolled through the gardens. A panther atop an elephant: the guests who were outside held their breath in amazement.

I took Ganesh to the water fountains so she could have some of my mother's fresh rose water. I had to be careful, as my mother never allowed me to do so because Ganesh made a mess. The fountains had faces carved into them—regal kings and gods, elephants and monkeys, and majestic horses. They spouted water from their heads and mouths into an open marble basin. The inhalation of fine perfumery was otherworldly and delicious; I learned these words from my mother. She made decadent attar perfume from it, which was likely why she didn't want Ganesh drinking it.

Moksha was running wild circles in the ring. He always had energy to burn, just like me. As soon as I approached him with Ganesh, he came near and started tossing his mane from side to side.

He wanted to be ridden.

"I know it's my birthday, but on this day, I think you deserve a treat, too. Well, you deserve one every day, like me." I giggled. "Yes, you do."

I slid down Ganesh's trunk and presented the squashed-up orange carrots. I guess it was a slight offering, as he ate them in one bite and looked at me with his signature look. It was as if he was saying: There must be more, right?

"I'm sorry, Moksha, but please do understand. I left the palace in a hurry to present this to you. I didn't have much time; I even had to sneak out. Next time, I promise I will bring more."

Looki followed me, meowing like I owed her more.

Teetu came rushing to me. "Rani, Rani, Rani, it is your party and you are having a party with the animals. I see where the true party animals are. Kabir is looking for you. He wants you to meet him on the rooftop, alone. He says he must speak to you under these auspicious stars."

"Okay, Teetu. I just need to grab a shawl. Please tell him I'm on my way."

I ran up to my room and laid a canvas out. I would paint this dream night upon it. I grabbed my grey cashmere shawl and ran to the roof—up two flights, and then two more secret flights to the roof.

"It is some party, is it not, princess?" The lines on his face spoke of his destiny even in the half-light of the crescent moon.

I was out of breath. I took a minute to inhale before I went to touch his feet in gratitude. "I'll tell you, baba, I am not as young as I was yesterday."

He laughed in pure bliss and delight.

"The humor on you cannot be replicated."

"The humor in me, you mean." I giggled.

"No, *on you*, as you are funny, too." We started to howl in laughter, and then I really howled to the moon, which he allowed me to do on my own. I think that this was a little too far gone for him.

The moment was eternally ethereal. One that could never be forgotten. Kabir was like the old wise djinn in ancient tales who appeared out of nothingness with a message or symbol that led and guided you to your beautiful fate. Everything about him was known to me. Nothing felt foreign or unknown. I never understood why he didn't move into the palace when my parents offered following his wife's death. But he always said that his home was where his queen once resided, for all of her breaths lived there—and that was his palace. He also spoke of how he lived within his temple; so, no matter where he was or where he went, he was home.

I dug into my panther pocket and reached for the painted box my father gifted me. This was the perfect moment: sitting with Kabir under the stars, destiny was written. Inside was the most dazzling six-pointed star cut from the finest diamonds cast in black and white; it was lined with sapphires around the tips of the star. It was a known talisman that could channel spirits and their forces through occult magic—channeling creation, balance, and the cosmos.

"Your father always said you were born from the stars."

"Oh, I just love it." Behind the star was another star made from lapis lazuli "the stone of the gods," the universal symbol of truth.

"This stone will protect you in all that you do. In any form of battle that life will throw at you, internally and externally. Use this as your guide, for vision and protection," Kabir advised. "I suggest that you wear it every day."

I held it up to the skies and a star beamed across the sky. I closed my eyes and sealed it with thoughts of guidance and protection. The star that shot across the sky disintegrated into the air, taking my wish with it.

"A sign—or what can I say?" Kabir commented.

"A sign it is," I answered.

"Never stop believing in your instincts of truth, of who you are and what you are. You took birth for a meaning decided upon by the gods. When and how that expires, you will be told. You were not born just to be a king's wife, but to love—that is your soul's purpose. Love changes the universe, love changes destinies, and love rewrites history. You have to know that all of us come here at certain times, for many different purposes. That's why we take so many births, so many lessons, and so many journeys to discover what is within. In this lifetime, you will be a woman of power, who commands much, makes many decisions, and leads the way with wisdom. You will do things that no other queen has done or that any woman has been given the opportunity to do. Use your truth wisely."

"What do you mean, Kabir?"

"Your husband will seek your guidance, so you must balance and prepare yourself for much responsibility and knowledge. To know what you are within so you can direct that energy with the proper intent. So, when the time comes, you can make decisions that are correct and in good conduct for all, not for self-interest or hierarchy."

I bowed before Kabir and went to look for my father. He was outside smoking beedi, a plant that seemed to make him loopy afterwards. As soon as he saw me, he opened his arms. "Come, come, come, my panther."

I gathered speed and jumped into his lion arms. They were quite long and strong, even though his shape didn't speak to a muscular structure. My mother always said he had the hands of a sorcerer.

I don't know how, but Kabir made it here before me. He always amazed and bewildered me. How he could just appear and disappear? Sometimes, I even wondered if he was real.

Akbar had a few of his advisors beside him. They all sat on plush cushions—which had Urdu poems sewn into them—atop the snow-white marble floor. They all looked a little loopy with their half-open eyes. Smoke hazes floated above their mouths with magic halos, and the sounds of the sitars vibrated from every angle of the living room. They discussed their enthrallment about the new laws for public hospitals that would change things for the betterment and health of all as they blew out smoke clouds.

Noble men they were.

I was getting a little loopy from the fumes. Not to mention that my eyes started to shut as I sat in lotus pose. Like a flower, I, too, wilted away into the night. My head lowered farther and farther, until I could feel my chin resting on my chest. A few head bobs later, my eyes opened and I bowed, even though I already fell asleep.

I sluggishly headed toward my bedroom, dragging my little body around the curves and swivels of the palace and up the spiral staircase. As I reached the top of the staircase, I heard my name being faintly called. I looked down and saw my mother with my half-open eyes.

She looked like a goddess even in my dreams.

"Good night, my little creature. I love you."

I lifted my leg and scrunched my arm like a cat. "Good night, my queen. Thank you. I love you," I whispered.

With that, I turned and walked into my bedroom. I was far too tired to change, so I crawled onto my sheets with tigers and elephants printed on them and let my panther self dream away.

When I awoke in the morning, I felt as though I slept for a decade. I wondered if the party was a dream. Even though I just turned 10, I could feel the changes my body was undertaking: slender curves were starting to appear, as well as new forms and indentations. I also was starting to get a lot more compliments on my features and how I was blossoming. Some who were my age were already married or procuring the necessary alliances and arrangements to do so. People would tell my parents how they admired my unique beauty and spoke of how my features were like none other. My eyes told a story dependent on my inner expressions and my cheekbones were set into the perfect position. My lips had a bold, blood-red hue; as well, they grew in size, like little pillows. My black mane flowed down my back and shone blue. Some compared my skin to gold, as it reflected the light.

I thought I should write the king a letter, telling him about what happened on my birthday. I recalled Kabir's words: "My child, this star is like no other star. This star, well, let me tell you about this star. There will be many doors and channels from visions that will come true from this stone, but only if you open your energy and listen to your instincts and allow your heart to lead the way. This star will protect you from dangerous liaisons. It will be your third eye. The only eye or 'I' you need."

He placed the star in between my eyes, on my third eye, and blessed me. "It is just as rare as you. Listen to the inner messages, for they will come."

I looked down at the star necklace and smiled. I signed my name with a star at the end and painted another on the ceiling. The stack of letters grew from a box to boxes, becoming a trilogy with a collection of paintings that followed.

त्रयोदशन्

Three years passed so quickly that time was untraceable. I was 13 and becoming someone new again. I looked wise beyond my years and my body had the silhouette of the feminine figurines I saw placed throughout the palace.

Daily, offers of marriage were presented to my parents by family, friends, aristocrats, and royalty. My parents poised and positioned me with a great many introductions, but none were the king. I knew it and boldly spoke it. Something within told me to wait and see—my star was silent and my third eye was closed to all as well. Kabir spoke of a timing and an age; there was still a year. My parents trusted that I would know when it was right. To be given such freedom was unheard of.

I channeled patience in meditation while I waited.

But on New Year's Day, a vision came to me in my dreams. Before, I daydreamed and fantasized at my own will, but this one came as an omen from the divine.

My hair, which fell far past my waist, was out of its braid and strewn across the bed. The blue diamonds on my hands glimmered like little cloud clusters. I looked outside at the magnificent trees and marveled at how their hands reached for the heavens. My father told me a tale of a friend who came from far away to visit and gifted my father with a seed to plant;

from that, it blossomed in the gardens of the palace into a tree worshipped by all. He said that the willow tree communicates with other trees and spirits through its roots. The universe and all that exists within it are all interconnected.

I looked at my ceiling of painted stars and knew that today I wouldn't draw a star. The gates of the gods had opened. I walked down to the gardens and saw my mother, Parwar, and my aunt Nur Jahan having their morning tea and treats.

"Good morning," I sang.

"Why, Arjumand, you are very dramatic this morning," my aunt replied. She was always a little dry and demure.

"Dramatic? Haven't I always been a storyteller through my emotions since birth?"

The three of them just laughed. My aunt had a laugh that seemed as though she rehearsed it well before. Maybe she did it so she could stand out from her new husband's, King Jahangir, thirty chief wives and countless mistresses. Everything about her was contrived. Her first husband, Sher Afgan, died a few years back. She always came to visit us; I think it was to break free from her nonexistent duties. She didn't have any, except to point her finger in whatever direction she wanted to order people around.

"And how are my queens and princesses this morning?"

"Swell," my sister replied.

"I think I am the same," my mother answered.

My aunt chimed in. "Just bashful, for look at where I am."

My mother smiled at her.

"Mother, I was wondering if I could go to the Meena Bazaar today. Parwar can accompany me if she likes. I would like to leave the palace and do some shopping—to see what it is they have to offer. I have a craving for something exotic and regal; who knows, I may decide to sell something as well."

"Regal? Is not all that you have regal? Just look around." My mother was puzzled.

"Of course, mother. It's just that I would like something new for New Year's. Parwar, would you like to join?"

"Oh no, not today. I have a great many needs to tend to today, and with the travels…it tires me so," Parwar answered.

My mother folded her arms and placed them flat against her stomach. She had an enviable figure. I guess all her years of yoga and only eating vegetables proved to be a winning recipe.

My aunt, on the other hand, liked to indulge a little too much and go for thirds. I guess with so much richness in her newfound life, she was used to hearing "yes," even when asking all the questions in her own mind.

"Well, your aunt and I have many preparations for tonight. Also, some guests are visiting this afternoon, so we cannot escort you. Let me see what I can conjure up."

"Thank you."

I grabbed a piece of Khamiri roti and ran off to my quarters. I watched my mother and aunt in the courtyard, laughing away, sipping their tea.

As the layers of clothing slipped off my skin onto the marble floor, I looked into the mirror at my body. This wasn't the same body I was born with. When I was little, I used to think that everyone around me was the age they were always going to be. I believed they would never change. But as I evolved, I saw that they did, too. My body also started to do things that only a woman's body did when you became a woman. I came to understand that everything was changing—constantly, minutely—even if my eyes didn't pick up on the details.

I filled the bath with the rose-water jugs. I love extreme heat for baths, but since I woke up late and engaged in conversation, I gambled away the heat. The black stone tile in my bath was designed with lovely intricate trees dipped in real silver that floated off of the most delicate branches.

After my bath, I rubbed coconut oil all over my body and massaged amla oil onto my hair roots. I decided to let it seep in while I looked at what I felt like becoming today. After looking at various garments in an arrangement of colors, pieces, and texturing, I decided I would close my eyes and see what came to me. I put my hand in my armoire and decided to do a twirl. I actually did two twirls, as I memorized my closet. I loved to memorize everything. I began doing this as a child because I thought I could take the images with me forever, even into the afterlife.

I heard a faint voice calling me from a distance, most likely on the other side of the palace. I put both hands in and closed my eyes, and then pulled out my black jewelled lehenga. It had tiny woven crescent moons and was covered in exquisite diamonds. A hilal or crescent moon was visible after a new moon, revealing the beginning or the end of a month.

How symbolic for the New Year.

I quickly put my star necklace back on.

I could now distinguish that it was Meera calling me. I rushed to the door and opened it just before she knocked, swinging the door open with a greeting.

"Yes."

I tried to inhale slowly so I could catch my breath.

"Arjumand." She looked me up and down. I hoped I put my lehenga on properly. "Your mother says Teetu can go with you, as everyone else is needed to prepare for New Year's dinner tonight or they have duties to attend to. But you must come back straight away after you have finished because we will have guests."

"Guests? What kind of guests?"

But I should meet him before. The thought raced through my mind and left a blueprint, a guide for me to follow.

"Oh, Arju, your mind is always in the clouds. You know what your mother's lavish festivities are about. How could I even begin to tell who would arrive? Teetu is ready when you are and the guards will follow behind." For a minute there, I thought it already began and I was there. That was until Meera spoke again and snapped me out of my dream world. "Come to the kitchen when you are ready. Teetu is waiting there."

I wrapped my arms around Meera and kissed her forehead. She smiled as she tried to break free. "Maybe you want to eat something? Let me know." The distant words echoed as she walked down the hallway.

I yelled after her. "Thank you. I love you."

I had a little time to add some color to my face and to play with my eyes. Painting my face was like the many brushstrokes I used to make one of the characters on my canvasses. I applied some kohl to my eyes and betel nut to my lips, staining them a faint ruby hue.

I slid my jhutis on and headed downstairs.

When I walked into the kitchen, Teetu was working away with Arjun. I decided to help and cut some vegetables for dinner while I waited. After a few minutes, Teetu caught on and locked eyes with me.

"You never announced you were here?"

"Well, when the time was right," I retorted, "I knew you would know. Besides, we have some time before we go and I know you have many preparations for tonight. Should you not know or see when a true queen appears and stands before you, then that is the issue."

With that, he sealed his agreement with a smile.

"Oh, queen *this*, queen *that*." He laughed.

The way I behaved with him wasn't how I acted with others. Around others there were proper formalities that needed to be maintained. I poured myself a cup of chai and worked my way to the okra, onions, and peppers. Why I chose to work with such fragrances before I went out, I didn't know.

"Ok, ready, ready. RRRRREEEEADY." He rolled his Rs and swung his nonexistent hips side to side. The staff was used to his theatrical behavior.

"Are you sure?" I asked.

"Yes, yes. Yes, I am, *maharani.*"

I followed behind him. Soon, two guards appeared. My father would have it no other way. They were dressed in jet-black trousers and long kurta tops with the family seal and crest on the upper-left corners by their hearts. Their camel leather jhutis were the shade of the desert sand. They bent and creased to the perfect formation of their feet.

"Today, we will go to the Meena Bazaar," I announced.

चतुर्दशन्

"Camel or horse? Which do you prefer, maharani?"

"Moksha is regal and Al Fahl is more rustic. Al Fahl will be best, as I have some goods to carry. Actually, how about both? I shall go on Al Fahl and come back on Moksha."

"Very, very good idea. I like your choice."

As they loaded the goods onto the other camels, I questioned the scarcity of what I brought. Well, there would be another time. I was already cutting it quite short.

The journey there took under two hours. However, everything that I saw and heard along the way through the villages enthralled me and pulled me toward ecstasy. I needed only to look behind and see lavish sand dunes and white plains, or straight ahead to a potter who dared not to blink as he stared at his wheel in a village. I loved the views from atop the camel and the breeze that fell upon my face.

The bazaar was tucked away on the outskirts of the city in Agra. An array of ruby-toned and pink fabrics covered the stalls of the outside vendors who weren't permitted to enter or sell inside the bazaar. It was said Akbar wanted to create the ambience from one of his palaces in Jaipur, also known as the

Pink City. At night and during the day, all the eye could see was a rose world, an exquisite bouquet of roses.

The sounds of bartering immediately excited me. I could spend hours gazing at one stall; and if I took a cup of camel milk with the owner, I walked out with their autobiography. Often, I got more inspiration for my creations from visiting the public stalls than the royalty market itself. It was a dimension of the past, present, and future—all within a moment.

"Where am I to begin?" I wondered.

"Begum Saahiba, what are you looking for? Let me help you. I have it all. What is your need?" one vendor queried.

"I'm just looking. I just got here, so nothing as of yet."

I moved Al Fahl back and forth until he resumed a seated position, hind legs tucked under. It was time for me to elegantly slide down, which was hard to do publicly.

I looked at Teetu as he and the guards were amused and entertained by a man with a grey flowing beard and turban. He had long fingers and nails, which foretold his practice of Tantra. His skin was so divine that it radiated the golden desert.

"I will be waiting, princess. Okay?"

"Yes, Teetu, thank you." I looked up at the sky and gathered my thoughts. "First, I think I will walk through, see what it is I desire. And if I should want anything, you will know."

"As you wish," Teetu replied and resumed his position back under the stall covering. I think he wanted more time with the comical, ghost-like villager.

The real bazaar started within the courtyards. Only royalty and nobility were allowed to enter. Women were permitted to sell and buy; kings and princes could only purchase. You could find everything inside the vaulted treasure chest—antique scriptures, vintage novels, otherworldly jewels, bejewelled hookahs, custom sculptures, commissioned art, and regal furnishings.

If a king could dream it, then it existed here.

I walked to the wooden doors inscribed with passages from the Quran. The silver calligraphy inscriptions were outlined in fine black, which made it look even more profound and dramatic. I was greeted by an array of guards who looked at my face in recognition and immediately proceeded to open the official palatial doors to the bazaar. It took six of them to open the doors, three on each side. A guard appeared and walked before me as I was presented, allowing for my formal introduction. I was now to leave the public forum and enter a world of privileged magnificence.

I always wondered how they could memorize so many faces. Then again, how could they not? Beautiful, elegant women walked about inside—few were granted the permission to do so. It felt like a kingdom within a kingdom. Carved trees depicted the faces of gods with candles lit inside and halos of clouds from the burning incense lingered in the air. Extravagant murals covered ever corner. I gazed at the first stalls and recognized some familiar faces among the women.

There was an abundance of jewels this time: emeralds, "tears of the moon," a great many diamond rugs, sarpeechs made from the most precious rubies, platinum archer's thumb rings made of hippo, precious gold flasks, crystal perfume bottles, regal turbans with ornate pin ornaments, and glamorous pendants.

Uniqueness permeated each creation.

As I made my way down the corridor, I saw some stalls that were cozy, while others bustled and burst. I had a profound love of antique books; my father gifted me that. A love of the poetic worlds. There was a book that caught my eye that a princess was selling on the Mughal Dynasty called "Ain-I-Akbari." It was written by Akbar's dear friend, Abul I Fazl, and recounted the administration of Akbar's reign. I was surprised to see the book, as it was very controversial. It even mentions a scandalous incident involving prostitutes and Birbal. It was said when Akbar heard such news, he wanted to punish Birbal, even though Birbal was known to be a spiritual man and was part of Akbar's courtiers called the "Navaratnas," or nine jewels. Abdul-Fazl, Raja Todoar Mal, Abdul Rahim Khan I-Khana, Faizi, Fakir Aziao-Din, Mullah Do-Piyaza, Raja Man Singh I, and Tansen were the rest. Akbar later came to know that the act was uncreditable, for many looked upon Birbal with envious eyes.

The words lingered on in print.

"Salam, how are you?" she asked.

"Lovely, thank you," I replied. "Where did you accumulate such a selection?"

"Well, these books have been in my family for many generations. My grandfather and father were lovers of the written word. Since there are far too many, my mother suggested we sell the ones we don't make use of. I'm Amira. My father is King Mirza. Akbar's my uncle. That's how I know about his intimate fondness of books, and how I acquired the book you are fond of."

"Knowledge is the kindest gift," I replied. "I think that I should set up a stall. You have given me quite the inspiration to do so," I confessed. "Come pass by if you have a moment later, Amira."

"See you soon," Amira responded.

"In-shallah, in God's wish," I spoke softly.

I peeked and peered into a few more stalls while making my way back to gather my things. As soon as the guards opened the doors, I was back in another dimension.

Teetu was slurping his camel milk chai.

"Teetu, I have decided that I wish to sell some things," I said. "Could you please arrange to bring me the goods?"

"Of course." He bounced up, eagerly waiting to serve. He started to wave his arms like Vishnu and dance, making it look like he was just summoning the guards and acting appropriately in public.

Teetu allowed me to carry the lighter packages I wrapped in cloth. He and the guards took the paintings and chests. The bazaar was congested. I didn't know how everyone appeared so quickly. Weaving in and out of bodies, my eyes eagerly searched for a vacant stall. The thought crossed my mind for a moment that there might not even be space for me now. We walked down to the very end, hoping a space was available.

To my surprise, there was.

"Teetu, this is the one, and the only one. We can place everything here."

"Yes, this looks good, Rani," he agreed.

With that, he was immediately off.

I didn't expect to sell much at all; therefore, I didn't have many things to unpack and display. I had a small selection of jewels and diamonds in a jewellery box, as well as a few paintings I created, which I hoped no one would question. There was also an antique statue of a Rajasthani maharaja on a horse and some classically painted plates in Victorian themes inside the chest.

I decided that the two paintings would be propped along the side edges of the stall, facing those walking by. I arranged the gems, diamonds, and jewels so that they looked like an offering floating off of the arms of the deity statues. I placed the necklace of sapphires around the base of the statue. In the east and south corners, I showcased the gold sarpeech headpieces; and in the north and west, I placed the ankle bracelets and porcelain plates. There was a rare blue diamond I wasn't certain if I should sell, so I kept it in my palm.

"How much is this?" a prospective buyer asked. A gold headband was wrapped around her fingers.

"Oh, I'm sorry. I didn't see you. Salam." I positioned my hands in prayer position.

"My daughter wants the gold headpiece."

"That one is two hundred Mohur coins."

"Do you want it?" she asked her daughter.

"Yes, I quite like it," her daughter replied. Her mother opened a yellow diamond-encrusted change purse and dropped the gold coins into my palms. The husband, who I didn't recognize, watched with little amusement.

"I have some silk I can wrap it in, if you like," I offered.

She nodded.

I ripped a piece of black silk into pieces and wrapped the headpiece, finishing it with a bow. She gestured a hand in prayer against her chest and smiled. She handed the black-bowed gift to her daughter and they were off. My next customer must have been a king, but I never met him before. He purchased the ultramarine sapphire necklace for one of his many wives; sometime later, he came back to buy the emerald-encrusted ankle bracelet for another.

It surprised me how much I sold in such a short duration. Soon, I wouldn't have much left to offer. All the women who stopped by the stall asked about the paintings: if they were antique, how much they were, who the king was, as well as many whispers and words that I couldn't hear.

I played along. "I don't know the famous artist's name; its age is unknown."

"What will it sell for?"

"I'm sorry. They are not for sale. I brought them just to share."

Paintings of the gods, fingerprints of the divine, the mystery of the unknown: those were some of the words spoken. There was a painting of the king staring at himself in the mirror, wrapping his black silk turban alongside his midnight stallion. In the other, the king read scriptures from the Quran while sitting under a blanket of stars and a crescent moon.

As time passed, many of the people began to disappear; most went to eat before the bazaar closed. I didn't have much of an appetite, so I stayed inside the stall. The food was otherworldly though, created by the finest chefs India ever produced. Many of the extravagant dishes and exotic cuisine treats were from faraway foreign lands and were never experienced before, even by those who led privileged lives.

पञ्चदशन्

I unclenched my fist and looked at the fine lines on my palm, releasing the icy diamond. I rolled it around, seeing if it could trace the lines of my destiny. I couldn't help but be taken away by its brilliance. I couldn't bring myself to sell it. Based on what I already sold, it would have been purchased right away. I don't know how to explain all these little stories that lived within my inner world.

My body temperature began to soar.

I could feel blood pulsating throughout my body. Intense bolts of electricity rushed down my astral spine; it was beyond surreal. Even though I sat in lotus pose, as still as a flower, my energy smoldered like fire and became uncontrollable.

A deep, strong voice whispered in my ear.

"What is it that you have in your hand?"

"In what hand?"

I squeezed my fist, unravelled my legs, and stood up. I couldn't even look up. I kept my eyes placed as they were—on my hands—even though the voice moved.

"In the hand you just closed," he responded.

I didn't open my fist to show what it was that I held. Instead, I nodded my head in acknowledgment. "Oh, it's not for sale."

I took a deep breath, one that he couldn't hear. I slowly gathered the courage to lift my eyes from the ground to see who asked the question.

And there he was before me...*the king.*

I couldn't believe my eyes. I didn't know if the diamond took me or if my paintings suddenly came to life—or if it was all just a fantasy. He was just as I envisioned.

How could that be?

How can you paint an image of perfection you've never seen? Is this why all the women stared at my paintings with such familiarity and knowing? His face was manifested by the universe's imagination—not even the most famous artist could have duplicated it if they tried. God must have taken my hand for every stroke, for I couldn't have created such mastery.

 He was elegant and exotic with deep-set almond eyes contrasted by fair skin and a strong chiselled jaw line that exuded his character and strength. Tales and heirlooms from long ago were bestowed upon him. He had all of the kings of the jungle on him. Yellow diamond necklaces cast as tigers and ruby rings born of panthers. Even as he stepped out of the light into the shade, their brilliance was just as intense. I looked down at the star necklace my father gifted me.

"It's not for sale," he murmured under his breath. I watched as he walked around and looked at the pieces for sale. Then, his eyes fixed on the paintings.

"It's not for sale," he stated again.

"It's not for sale," I repeated.

Even when things weren't for sale, if a king requested it, it was almost mandatory to feed his every craving. He stared at the painting; actually, he gazed right through it. Noticing the resemblance, he took a step back.

"Who is this?" he asked.

I didn't respond, thinking that he knew.

"What king is this?" he asked again.

Again, I didn't respond.

"Is it an antique? Oh, let me guess, princess: it's not for sale. Is nothing in this stall for sale?" He laughed.

"Some things are," I assured him. "Just not the things you are inquiring about. This piece is." I gestured to a carving. "And so is this piece. The diamond in my hand is for sale as well, but I don't think you can afford it. That's why I took it off the market."

"You took it off the market before we discussed a price, princess? What kind of business is that? I must say that I do love how you think. That is the most amazing tactic I've ever heard of: to entice one with what he wants when you have it. I shall try it elsewhere myself to see if it has such effects," he mused. "Besides your beauty, I see you also have a complex mind. Deadly combination, I must say. Let's not forget, you're mysterious as well. May I ask what makes you think that I cannot afford what dazzles in your palm? Please do tell."

"I can tell you, but I won't tell you. I don't know why I think such thoughts."

"I see you like games, as well as riddle and rhymes."

I could feel perspiration dripping down every crevice of my body. I had never felt as alive as I did in this moment, so much so that new cells and life introduced themselves instantaneously.

"Please indulge me. Give me a price, as we already know I cannot afford such gems," he teased.

I stared into his eyes, looking for an answer.

"10,000 Mohur coins," I blurted out.

The Mohur gold coin weighed 10.95 grams and was introduced by Sher Shah Suri in 1540. Even I was quite shocked to hear such an exorbitant amount slip through my lips. I knew that when he heard such a price, he would definitely think I was out of my mind.

"10,000 gold coins for your diamond?"

"There are few untouched, flawless blue diamonds like this. And this one is special and rare, for reasons I do not care to disclose. I have stated what I think is fair," I proclaimed.

"And if I pay that, princess, will you sell it to me?"

I kept staring into his eyes.

I couldn't break his hypnotic gaze.

I found my reply in his eyes. "I will sell you the diamond, as that is a lot for charity. And I believe that this stone will be a blessing for you as well. Seeing as you are a king, I'm sure you would think such an amount is nominal, especially when it comes to giving to our people."

"But you say I cannot afford it?" He smiled.

"Well, that is if you can pay such an amount," I replied. "*Can* is always the magical word."

With that, he turned around and walked down the corridor, whistling. One of his men rushed from the entry doors, panting and out of breath. I suppose no one makes a king wait.

After a few moments, he walked back.

"The painting is not for sale?" he questioned.

"No, the painting is not for sale. We did not discuss it, nor is there any reason to do so, as I won't change my mind."

"May I ask, what is your name?"

I looked down at the floor and slowly eyed his body until I met his eyes. They were locked on me all along. "My name is Arjumand Banu. And who are you?"

"Who I am has many layers and many meanings, but my name is Shah Jahan. Maharaja Shah Jahan. To some, for now, Prince Khurram."

"Well, I'm Princess Arjumand." I smiled. "Soon-to-be queen is what our seer Kabir told us—but for now I'm a princess, even though not by title."

"I see that, maharani. Well, I'm sorry, you are right. I do not have 10,000 golden Mohurs, not even close. It's as though you knew before we spoke. Do you have psychic visions? Maybe mystical powers?"

"Well, I am known for predicting things and foretelling the future. My seer did speak of such gifts."

"Oh, so I should bestow gifts upon you, like a god, if you have such powers?"

"You cannot even afford the 10,000 Mohur coins. How can you do more?"

"Not all gifts are shiny tokens," he noted. "Some are from the soul and those are priceless."

He turned and walked out of the stall, not looking back as he left. I watched as he walked to the main doors, making sure that he didn't see me. I slipped back into my stall, knowing he would be back.

I patiently sat in lotus pose, pretending to meditate.

"10,000 gold coins? Give me a moment please. Let me see how many it is that I have in here."

I couldn't see what was inside as it faced him, nor did I want to seem too inquisitive. He looked at me after he finished counting. "Okay, yes, but barely. That looks like the right amount. You can make a king poor with your beauty."

I didn't even want his money.

I just wanted more time with him.

"Please open it," he said.

I walked over and placed my hand on the golden heart-shaped lock and unlocked it. As I lifted the chest's lid, my eyes felt as though they were turning into gold. I never saw so many coins. The blinding golden tokens with faces of great kings were double-stamped and covered every inch and surface.

"I'm giving you 100,000. As you say, it is for charity. How could I not?" he declared. "And the paintings, how can I find the artist?"

I didn't know how to answer.

The paintings.

"Well…well, that would be me."

"Princess, I have known that all along."

With that, he turned and walked away.

षोडशन्

I looked at my sundial; dusk was approaching. This meant I would have to get going. I couldn't be late for dinner. I walked over to the chest and tried to lift it, but could not. I tried attaching a silk tie and pulling it, but the fabric broke. He must have even more strength than I imagined. I roared like a tiger, albeit a silent tiger, and ground my teeth. I put all of my bodyweight into it and it didn't move. I left the chest in the far corner, draped a shawl over it, and went to call for Teetu.

He was engaged in the same conversation and drinking his umpteenth chai, as if I never left. I whistled to get his attention. Finally, he turned around. "Oh sorry, dear, he had such funny jokes that I didn't see you." He slapped his leg as tears streamed down his face. "Here is the joke, princess. Why is man living the life of a camel? Because his life, too, has many humps."

I couldn't help but join in with his fits of laughter. The joke wasn't funny, but Teetu was. His laugh was contagious, along with his overt gestures.

"Okay, princess, how can I help you?" he asked, drying his tears while still smiling at his friend. "Are you done inside?"

"Yes, Teetu, I need a hand lifting the goods."

With that, he turned to the man and twirled his hands to the sky in a typical Indian gesture to close their conversation. "Princess, did you sell many things?"

"Teetu, you will never believe it."

"Believe what? What? Come on, princess, tell me!"

"We must keep our voices down. I don't want anyone to hear what I say. I will show you. Come to the stall."

As we entered the stall, he looked around in pure confusion.

"Was it very slow?"

"No, no. I just didn't have many things to sell—just some jewels and such. And some things I did not want to sell."

He started to laugh again, uncontrollably. "You open a stall and say 'no' to selling." He hit his knee again. "Let me be princess. You be customer. Welcome to my stall," he said in a girlish voice.

"Hi, I'm just looking. Thank you," I replied. "Oh, this shawl. How much is it?"

"It's not for sale," he said. "Nothing is for sale in this stall. You open a stall to sell goods to kings and nothing is for sale." He started to shake his fingers like they were firecrackers, and then exploded in giggles.

"I see." I laughed as well.

"We should prepare everything promptly so we can get you home on time, princess. You always get me in trouble with your idea of time."

"Yes, but first I must show you something, Teetu. Have a seat on the cushion."

He propped himself on it, acting like a customer.

"Teetu, lift the shawl," I directed.

"Okay, I will lift shawl."

"Okay, unlock the lock."

"Open your heart and turn the key, says princess."

His mouth dropped open; he froze. I had never heard him so silent before. "Oh, my good God, Allah, and Vishnu. What happened here? What did you sell? Who gave you this?"

I peered out of the stall again to make sure no one was coming. "The king gave me this," I whispered.

"A king gave you this to get married? He offers to buy you here? Does he not know you cannot buy a princess at a bazaar? This is not 1200. This is how much he thinks a princess is worth? Oh no, no, no, no." He shook his head.

"I'm worth more than that. We both know."

He slapped his thigh, "Oh, princess, gold cannot equate to your worth, but maybe diamonds," he teased, winking. "Only the rarest ones, too."

"Speaking of diamonds, remember the blue diamond that father gifted me? Well, I thought I might sell the piece and donate the money. But when I came here, I became even more attached to it and just couldn't bear to part with it. While I was gazing at it, the king appeared and saw it in my palm. He inquired about its price. I told him that it was too expensive. And instead of the 10,000 gold coins I stated as its price, he gave me 100,000. He wanted to buy my paintings, but those I could not sell, even for 100,000 gold coins."

"You painted these?" Teetu asked. "I have seen a great many of them in your room."

"I knew that he was the king I was to marry, even though I never met or saw him before. Don't ask how or why, but when he walked in, I knew. It's my timing from the constellations."

"You just met. How do you know he is the *king?*"

"I do. I know."

I took a few of the Mohur coins from the chest and gave them to Teetu. I tucked a few away for the guards.

"Princess, I am trying, but I cannot lift this. I need help."

Teetu went to fetch the guards. When they returned, one of the guards bent down to lift it. "What is in here?" he growled.

"Oh, just metal." I smiled at Teetu.

Before we were to set foot, I gave Al Fahl some water for the journey home, as I could see that his hump was deflated by the humid dry air. Teetu saw me doing this and began laughing as he stared at the hump.

My face was profusely sweating from the smoldering sun. The brazen sun created quite a love affair with my garments, which ended in heat engulfing me. My skin yearned to feel fresh air from the mask of sweat beads that had accumulated upon my skin; my mane lusted for a breeze.

"Teetu," I yelled. "Let's ride through the barren lands before we go home."

"Yes, princess."

I watched every detail of life that passed me as I rode Moksha. My life had changed within a moment. It was as though I stepped into a world of the unknown after I met him.

My life would never be the same.

I wanted to play, so I had Moksha do circles around the peepal trees. I loved it when he would go up on his hind legs and I would have to hold onto his mane for dear life as he galloped as fast as he could around the trees. Teetu's eyes always bulged out of his sockets when I did so. I don't know who he trusted less—me, the horse, or both.

"Okay, princess, only a little more. Soon, we must go home," he cautioned.

"I know, I know. Home," I acknowledged.

With that, I put my hair back into an orderly fashion, hiding my previous bouts of wildness from the world once again. "We must go back, so we must be calm, Moksha," I soothed.

He bowed his head in acknowledgment and started to trot. I really got him going: his wild heart pumped so vigorously that it vibrated right through my legs and up my spine to my heart.

The guards spoke amongst themselves as we stood outside the palace gates awaiting entry. My father always kept the quickest and sharpest guards at the gates and the strongest ones for defense inside. That was his strategic plan for protection that I learned as a child.

"Teetu, can you please bring the chest to my room?"

"Yes, I will tell the guards."

"Oh, and please give these to them," I said, placing the gold coins in his palm. "Thank you."

"How was your day?" my mother yelled from the kitchen. I stopped on the first step of the marble stairway and walked down so she could hear me.

"It was lovely. Much to do and a lot to see. What time is dinner?"

"In a few hours. Remember, tonight we will have many guests."

I ran up to my room and saw the chest was already there. I ripped off my lehenga, put on my white sheath, and draped a shawl to provide more coverage and modesty. I then made my way downstairs to the kitchen.

"Where is father?"

"I think he's in the courtyard having tea."

"Thank you."

I ran down the hallway, out the front doors, and down the walkway to the courtyard. My father was having chai with other men seated on camel-bone chairs. They were surrounded by the lush greenery of the gardens. As I approached him, I slowed down so I could catch my breath. I bowed to the floor and touched my father's feet.

"Arjumand, how are you? You're running so fast. From who and what?" he chuckled.

"Water please." He poured me an ice-cold glass from the clay jug, which was flavored with the essence of oranges.

I looked up and smiled. "The bazaar was wonderful."

"Did you sell many gods?" he asked.

"You mean goods?" I laughed.

"Oh gods, goods, they all come from God. We were just talking of such matters. My mind is still there."

"I have something to show you. Do you have a moment to spare so you can step away?"

"You can't bring it here?"

The guests smiled at him, an indication that they were comfortable with him stepping aside and interrupting the discussion. "Please give me a few moments."

As we walked to the house, I walked in unison with my father. "What is it?" he queried. "Did you buy something? That tiger you wanted?"

"No father, not a tiger. I have to find my tiger, not just any tiger. Besides, I have never seen one for sale at the bazaar."

I loved being close to my father. I cherished every moment that I was near him. I made sure that I didn't attract the attention of the others; I wanted my father alone. While walking up the stairs, I could tell my father's curiosity grew with each step he took. I was never one to pull my father away or to need him at a moment's notice.

I turned the key to unlock my bedroom. I think my father wondered what might jump out at him. What was I hiding? What secret?

His eyes spoke that he saw nothing different.

"Okay, please have a seat."

He obediently sat at the edge of my bed on the carved wooden elephant trunks that served as legs. The headboard had an elephant's face, with ears that came out and acted as end tables.

"Father, today I took some things to the bazaar—one of them being the blue diamond you gave me."

"And you sold it? Arjumand, that one is lovely. A gem of fine-quality carats: the clarity and cut are superior. Did you get a good price?"

"You see, well, I didn't want to sell it, since you gifted it to me. In my eyes, it was different and unique. I sold an assortment of things, but held off on that piece. Then, a king walked by and saw it glimmering in my hands while I thought it was hidden; he offered to buy it. I rejected his offer. And then I said I would sell it for 10,000 Mohurs."

"10,000 Mohurs?" He was amazed. "That is quite the amount, Arjumand. It is worth 6000."

"Yes, I know, but that's why I told him such a price. I changed my mind; I didn't wish to sell it." I walked over to the trunk and slowly unlocked it.

My father stood up from his seat, anxious to see what it held. Carefully, I cracked the chest open, inch by inch, until it was exposed. I turned around just in time to catch the expression on my father's face.

"But he gave me this."

"Arjumand, how much is this?"

"100,000, all for charity. Well, maybe 99,994. I gave a few away."

"But how? How many pieces did you sell?"

"Just the blue diamond."

"How could the king not know its worth? Did he not ask or seek his financial advisor before he paid you?"

I unfolded the story of my transaction to my father and kept the romance, and my undying love for the soon-to-be king, out of it.

"You should work for me," he said with a laugh. He looked around my room in awe. Within a moment things had changed and there were things he never saw before. That was when he saw the paintings strewn about. "And the paintings?" he asked. "Who created these?"

"Oh, lately I have been painting all sorts of things. For quite some time actually. It just that now I have started to display them."

"Quite the artist you've become. One day, these will go down in history. The Shah must have loved your diamond." He looked at me with a grin, like he knew, but didn't probe.

"I will ask the guards to deliver this so it can be donated. You did well. This will help a great many," he noted as he kissed my forehead. "I will see you at dinner, for I must go back. Money doesn't come so quick for me. Soon, I shall work for you, your Royal Rani. I love you, Arjumand."

"I love you, too," I replied.

There was a knock at the door. Two stiff knocks, one after another: they never changed their knocks.

"Please take the coins, but bring back the chest and lock."

"With certainty."

"Thank you."

I went down to the kitchen.

"Perfect timing, Arjumand. Your sister is setting the table. Can I ask you and Teetu to cut flowers and place them?" my mother asked.

"Of course we can," Teetu responded.

"Were there many things at the bazaar?" my mother asked.

"So many beautiful and different things for the New Year. I saw a great many things I've never seen before, even though everything there is already quite rare."

"That is great, more for charity. Did you sell anything?"

"A few items and a diamond."

I looked over at Teetu and smiled, putting a finger to my lips to shush him before he revealed my private escapades. "Come Teetu, let's cut some flowers."

"Why didn't you say anything?" he asked as he looked at me through the rose bushes.

"Because I want to see what the universe does. What happens next," I revealed. "Besides, I haven't told anyone but you."

"Your mother will be so excited," he said. I think he liked this game of clipping flowers and talking to me through the greenery.

I walked out from behind the bush so I could make direct eye contact with him. I looked around and made sure no one else was nearby. "Now isn't the time. Promise me that you won't say a word about anything," I pleaded.

"Do I ever say anything, maharani?" he teased.

"I'm not a queen yet. Maybe we should cut some tulips, roses, and marigolds."

"As you wish. As you wish."

"As I wish? I shall," I replied.

I knew it: oh no, riddles and rhymes. This would encourage him to break into song and dance, singing to the gods about how they could wish and wish, and that we all shall—especially since no one was around. He really was in his own world.

As I cut the last rose, I started to bunch them together and tie them with the magenta silk ties. Teetu's creations were breathtaking. He incorporated every color, from the palest shades of nudes to blood pink in the center—to magical black roses on the outside. All of Teetu's gestures were an expression and expansion of who his spirit was in that moment.

We placed two bouquets on opposite sides of the doors, and then Teetu went around placing various ones in different locations. I went to the dining room to design my display as my mother directed me.

The elegant main dining room seated a few hundred guests and I knew that all of the seats were spoken for. My father would sit at the head of the table with my mother to his left; Parwar and I would sit to his right.

"Arjumand? Where are you?"

"Here in the dining room, mother."

"Oh, there you are. What a beautiful setting you have made." She gazed at my decor, taken away by the heavenly aroma that lingered in the room. Flowers were the fragrance to her soul.

"You should dress. I need you to wear your best garments. We know how you like to take your time getting ready and daydreaming in between."

"Yes, I do." I scattered the excess rose buds in the bowls around the room and turned to leave.

"Oh, Arjumand."

"Yes, mother?"

"Please brush your hair. I got you that horse-mane brush, so I know you will use it."

"I know, mother. I will try to brush my hair and show up in my best garments."

Inside, I giggled uncontrollably.

A princess who rides stallions, didn't brush her hair, and wore kurta pyjamas all day; I did what most wouldn't dare to do. I had a different thought for each step to my bedroom. I propped myself on my bed to let my imagination wander for a while.

I was blessed to have parents who always encouraged me to be me. They never asked me to dim or turn off my light; they wanted me to be just as I was—as my father said, "Like the sun." Who shines and exists, even when it isn't seen. And because of that, I was allowed to commit to my choices and risks in life of who and what I wanted to become. I did not seek explanations or permission from others for who I was. There was no need for validation from outside sources. I was complete just as I was…perfect the way the gods created me.

The water Teetu put in the tub was warm. I put my hands on the jugs of water by the tub: they were hot. I would use those to get the desired heat. Delicate rose petals floated atop the water, while the coconut oil competed for space. My body quickly absorbed all of the nutrients it lost during the day. Some of my chakras were closed, perhaps due to travel and the long day. It was quite a spectacle for me to leave the palace.

I stood up in the tub and started to do vriksasana (tree pose), as my favorite place besides the gardens to do yoga was in the bath. I love trees for their symbolic meaning of selflessness and how they communicate with one another— giving to all, even when others harmed them. One tree supplies enough life for four people; four people they may never even know. Life was deeply connected within me through my veins like the roots of trees.

I sat down and closed my eyes and put my hands into different mudras, channeling Padma Mudra for unconditional love. Each breath invoked a new being in me and slowly I inched my entire body under water, until finally my head was submerged as well. Being underwater, even for just mere moments, was freeing.

The sun dimmed behind the villages and it covered the area to the east: that meant it was 7:17.

I had less than an hour.

My mother was right.

I did spend more time fantasizing than I realized. I wrapped my hair into a turban so it would dry quicker. As I looked into the mirror, a thought filled my mind. *I must have been a king at one time.* My features were quite androgynous depending on my inner expression—who or what it was that I wished to portray. I could transport myself into a multitude of identities just by shifting my energy.

सप्तदशन्

The signature two knocks at the door informed me that it was time to get dressed. Everything was timed and calculated when an important function was afoot, right down to the minute.

"Arjumand, your mother is asking if you are ready."

"Almost," I spoke through the door. "I'm changing now. Please tell her." I sat in front of the mirror and started to brush my hair. I built a side plait since my hair was still wet—and I needed a disguise. I put some crushed berries on my lips and lined my eyes with kajal, smudging it a little with my fingertips. I laid my lehenga on the bed and went to my chest and pulled out my velvet and lattice-embroidered cape. I felt that was where magicians would place theirs, if they had one. Keeping it there would also retain its luck.

As I put the garments on, I could feel the universe changing and shifting. I assumed a regal and royal demeanor that was far more refined and contained than my usually expressive self. As I looped the side tie on my skirt, I peered out the window and saw guests walking up to the entrance; others descended from their various modes of transport. I decided that because my lehenga skirt was long enough, I didn't need to wear shoes.

As soon as I opened the door, Parwar was there.

"Perfect timing. Shall we?"

"I believe we are on time, Arjumand."

I smiled faintly, closed the door, and followed behind her. I looked down from the staircase and could see familiar and unfamiliar faces. Dinner was going to be larger than I expected.

"Oh my, look at you and your sister. I haven't seen you since the last, well, was it not the horse chase?" That was our first introduction to the guests of the evening.

"You mean horse race," I quipped.

"You are right, Arjumand. How are you?"

"I'm well, amme." We called the elder females *aunt*. Considering I couldn't remember her name, I thought a respectful gesture would suffice.

"Amme Zharani, how are you?"

My sister always had a way with names; I went by faces or how much I actually cared to remember them. Zharani, Zharani: I ran it through my brain like a memory zap, hoping I would remember next time.

Nope, I wouldn't.

"Excuse me."

With that, I put my hand on my sister's shoulder, leaving her to converse with the woman I never seemed to remember.

Teetu was busy singing away to the clay oven and finishing off the last preparations for dinner. My father called for a few dozen more helpers today, as feasts like this took a lot of tending to. I looked inside the delicate glass jugs to see what kind of juice there was. I noted three varieties that I recognized from our fruit trees in the garden—mango, lychee, and amla. I thought I would try the amla.

"Oh, no, no, down," Teetu said.

"No, no, down, Teetu?"

"Look what you have on, my queen. You want to drink amla juice? Knowing how you are the staining and dripping type, maharani."

"I'm a staining maharani?"

"Oh, princess will be a queen soon."

"Is that a guess?"

"Not all princesses become maharanis, but you have always been a queen, even when you were a princess because of your heart."

I hugged Teetu and saw that he was struggling to hold onto the jug so it wouldn't fall with the suddenness of my hands wrapped around him. "I'm different today. I can be trusted with such things. Just watch."

"Careful, careful. Okay, you go to the main room. I will bring this for you."

"But how do you know which one?"

"I know. I know," Teetu reassured. "Now go. I have eyes. Your mother wants you there. She is waiting."

I smiled and nodded at the faces that consumed what were once empty spaces of the palace. I could smell a wide variety of jasmine and patchouli incenses as I floated down the hall, allowing for them to lead the way.

"Arjumand."

I looked behind me and saw my uncle.

I remembered his name. I loved him.

I ran up and gave him a huge squeeze.

"Wow, you are one peaceful warrior! No wonder I will take you with me as my right hand, wise one. How have you been? Your mother says you have been doing yoga and riding Moksha. How is Moksha?"

"Oh, he's delightful—well, a little crazy and wild."

"Oh, so he is just like his master." My uncle broke out into a fit of laughter. The surrounding guests turned to look at him; his laugh was such that it made it seem like he just heard the funniest joke ever. His nostrils would flare, his pudgy cheeks would redden, and he would slap his protruding stomach.

I laughed in a ladylike manner, as he had a very contagious energy about him. He waved his hands to the guests, like he was some sort of royalty, and bowed. They smiled back and laughed, resuming their conversations.

"So, Arjumand, I am going to tiger-taming classes. I told your father I know how badly you want one. Maybe you can join and see how your uncle tames the tiger."

"You are taking classes to tame a tiger? How are you taming a tiger?"

With that, he put his hand in mid-air like a tiger and clawed at the air, and then pointed to himself. "I am taming this tiger," he declared. He then kissed me on my forehead. "You tell your father you want to go and I will arrange it, even though it's men only. We can dress you up, disguise you once again." He winked to solidify our secret plan.

"I will. Thank you."

"Arjumand." I heard my mother's voice calling me from down the hall.

"I will come back later," I promised my uncle. "Mother's calling."

"Come back, don't come back; leave, don't leave: you're still my favorite," he noted.

As I walked past the guests, I smiled and greeted them with bows and my hands in the prayer position.

"Oh, there you are."

"Yes, here I am, mother."

"You look beautiful. Like a goddess," my mother observed. "I was wondering why so many were speaking of you and telling me of your whimsical and godlike beauty. And I wondered how you decided to paint yourself today. Now, I see such a vision. Your aunt is looking for you."

"Oh, is she?" I responded.

I looked around, but I couldn't see her.

"Maybe she is in the gardens. You may want to check there."

"I shall go there, mother."

As I walked down the hallway, I could see Teetu running with a glass of juice, which spilled over the rim because of his rapid and abrupt movements.

"Okay, close your eyes," he demanded.

I closed my eyes and he placed a cold glass in my hand.

"Guess which one. What flavor is this?"

"Well, knowing you and how you know me, I would say the amla."

"Oh, you know me too well, Arjumand. Try it. Tell me if it's tasty."

I took a sip. It immediately melted down my throat. It was the most invigorating vitamin juice, made with the soothing essence of the bittersweet super-fruit amla and refreshing mint that added a zing.

"Words can't even express such a delicious flavor."

I slowly walked through the gardens in search of my aunt. In doing so, my eyes were taken away in wonder, as there was something to see in every direction. Mother made sure there was an array of entertainment from every realm so the guests always had something to be amused by. My parents liked to invite a variety of souls—dramatic, plain, old, and young. Just like the assortment of dishes and recipes being served.

Just as I turned the corner, Vishnu, my peacock, appeared and stood before me. In Hindu scriptures, peacocks are a symbol of the cycle of time, as well as heaven and earth. The peacock was created from one of the feathers of Garuda, the transcendental bird carrier of Lord Vishnu. Though Garuda had the head, wings, talon, and beak of an eagle, he possessed the body of a man. It was said that Garuda's wings chanted the Vedas when he flew and he was so powerful that he could block the sun.

Vishnu's intense eyes stared through me. The eyes on his feathers were doing so as well. I knew what this meant. He liked my costume and thought this was the time for a battle of the fancy feathers. Clearly, my garment commanded too much attention for his palette.

Vishnu's story was quite enchanting.

He mysteriously appeared and strolled through the palace as if he owned it, unannounced and uninvited. He then decided to sit in the gardens for days admiring his reflection in the canals. There were times when I would look for him and I couldn't find him—sometimes for days on end. He would just disappear; and other times, he would just appear. I often wondered if he was a figment of the palace's imagination. But since everyone else claimed to have seen him, I knew he must be real.

That's who he was, visible and invisible.

When I wore something that sparkled or shined, he made it a point to show who had the better costume. He took a few steps back and revealed every layer and coloring from his elaborate wingspan—from sky-blue turquoise to hunter greens and silver greys. His feathers unfolded a story of vibrant forecasts and exotic views as he paraded in circles around me, letting me know that he was the best dressed. I bowed before him, a sign that I was waiting for him to dance. His feathers floated in the air and moved to every beat of his dance. I could tell that he knew I wasn't the only set of eyes watching him.

He made sure of it.

It was known that as soon as a gifted feather fell, he was done; the Vishnu show was over. I picked up the psychic feather and thanked him. He turned and walked away, knowing that I was still watching his every move in awe. It was an unspoken rule that I wasn't allowed to break my gaze until he left my sight.

I saw my aunt by the fountains, sipping chai and chatting away. She, too, watched Vishnu's spectacle. "Arjumand, please come here," she called.

"I'm coming."

"Arjumand, my friend Diya was commenting on your beautiful design and I told her you designed it. Diya came all the way from Delhi for your parents' dinner," my aunt continued. "Her daughter is getting married soon."

"A pleasure to meet you," Diya responded.

I couldn't break my gaze from her eyes. I felt as though I was in a hypnotic trance. Her name must have been a hint, as Diya meant splendor and radiance.

"How old are you, Arjumand?" she asked softly.

"I'm 14."

"Will you be married soon?"

"Yes, very, very soon," I promptly replied.

My aunt looked at me quizzically.

"My daughter is your age. She is to marry King Abdahalla next year, April 17th—the date the astrologer and pundit have prescribed. And you, when will you?"

"I shall be with him soon," I revealed. "But my engagement will be a lot longer."

My aunt looked bewildered. "With a great deal of suitors and such beauty, I know we will have a hard time choosing which prospect, but we are doing so now. But with her heart, we need the perfect key."

Did she know what happened today at the bazaar? Had she heard? But how? I kept my face neutral the whole time, so as not to give anything away.

"Excuse me. There are a few things I must tend to. Diya, it was a pleasure and I thank you for coming all this way. I look forward to your daughter's wedding."

My feet started to unexplainably walk. It was as if they had a mind of their own. They moved with their own agenda, skimming atop the grass. I had no control. I walked up the marble stairs of the palace's entry. When I got to the last step, my instinct was to immediately turn around. But my feet were planted firmly. My back still faced the guests.

Slowly, I moved my feet like clockwork while staring at the floor. I must have looked like a delicate puppet being pulled ever so cautiously by her puppeteer. I was at the 21th hour now, but I would have to get to midnight. Even though it was just a step away, it felt like eternity.

I commanded my left foot to its final destination and my eyes to gaze toward the heavens. After a few moments, and once I gathered enough courage, I peered over the balcony. And at that very moment, he looked up and his eyes locked with mine. The timing was so synchronistic that it must have been calculated by the gods. Our gaze didn't break, nor did the flood of incarnations that we shared in silence.

His silk cloud-white kurta pyjamas had golden zari stitching and intricate embroidery. Rubies and gems were purposefully placed; they reflected all that was around him. Polki diamonds and pearls were beaded into his ornate turban.

I tried to lift my tingling toes, but I became a cement figurine. I was now a statue. All I could do was center my breath. He jumped off his magical carrier and walked over to the elephant, holding out his hand. A woman descended down the ladder. The elephant had ornate colors painted on its wise grey skin, a mural of the gods Shiva and Parvati in matrimonial bliss.

Who was she?

He turned to me and smiled, knowing that my eyes remained on him, but also letting me know that even if his eyes moved, or left mine, he was always watching me. His eyes were from another world—for they truly were the window to his soul.

Eyes that did not need words to speak.

The guests were formally guided to the palace's entry, but he lingered behind. I kept questioning if I should join and follow behind as they entered, as I never behaved in such a manner before. But I believed he was waiting for a moment of privacy for us, and for that I would wait an eternity.

He personally gave his horse water, but the workers ran to take over. It looked as though he was conversing with his horse, which I found very peculiar. I had never seen such behavior before, except when I did so myself.

I anxiously waited to see what unfolded next.

He made his way toward the stairs. Each and every breath I took henceforth became shorter and shallower in anticipation of his arrival. My only clue was the sound of his clicking heels on the marble. They sounded like diamonds being dropped—not overpowering or pronounced, but delightful.

He was two steps away.

Where was he?

I waited in confusion.

I didn't look up.

Where did he go?

He should be here; it was only two steps. I wanted to look, but I dared not. I waited for what seemed like a lifetime and finally decided I would sneak a peek. He jumped two steps silently, knowing that I was anticipating his arrival.

I was fooled.

I stood there in a coy manner, knowing our closeness wasn't permitted—not for me at least. He confidently came next to me and gazed upon the gardens.

"It's been a long journey here and the heat has been excruciating all day…as you know. But who would have known that what lays before my eyes is what my mind has been imagining since."

I didn't respond.

I just looked at him.

He spoke again. "Are you stashing away more diamonds from the constellations? You seem as though you are sitting atop the clouds. Or maybe above the sun, as it seems the heavens bestow its radiance upon you. Is that how you gathered such beauty?"

The doors of the palace opened. I recognized the guards by their wrists and cuffs even before their bodies appeared. I stepped away from the king just in time. A man stormed out to greet the king. I discreetly moved farther away to avoid untoward suggestions.

"Look who is here. Come inside," he told the Shah, leading him into the palace. As they walked toward the doors, I overheard the king speaking of a thirst. I watched as he became a faint shadow walking down the hallway.

And then suddenly he stopped and looked at the floor. Gliding his hand into the pocket of his pyjama pants, I saw a glimmer of my diamond appear. He placed it in his palm and closed it the way I did at the bazaar.

I weaved my way in and out of guests, searching for Teetu. He was quite difficult to find on such occasions, partly due to his height and also the fact that he was always here, there, and everywhere.

The kitchen would be my next stop. When I got to the kitchen, Teetu was busy putting the final garnishes on the plates. "Princess, do you need a job?"

"Of course, that's why I'm always here. Teetu, I'm just going to pour a glass of juice."

"As you like, it's all for you."

"Teetu, would you like to do something for me?" I waved my hand, motioning him over so I could speak to him without the others hearing. I put my hand over his ear, leaned in, and whispered. "Teetu, Teetu, you won't believe it. He's here."

"Who is here, Rani?" he said loudly.

"The purpose of this is a secret. Lower your voice please." I gestured by covering his ears with my hands. "Can you not tell by my whispering?"

"You're right," he said, as if he was pondering it.

"Teetu, the king is here. I want you to serve him the juice I had, as I heard he is thirsty." I spoke the rest so quickly that most of my words were most likely lost. "He's wearing a white silk kurta pyjama with gold stitching and a pearl and diamond turban. He has high cheekbones and deep dark eyes that have a panther-like essence. His lips are like…"

"Okay, okay, princess, enough. No more details. I'm sure I can tell by the kurta. This is the king, as in the *king*? The Bazaar King?"

"Yes, I think he may be in the formal seating area, but I didn't want to go there and see."

"Okay, I will go. I will serve him his juice."

He grabbed the jug and mimicked as if he was serving his majesty, bowing his head and pouring it to perfection. I wanted everything I gave to the king to have been touched by me. That's why I poured it.

"Here it is. Please take it to him, Teetu."

"On my way now. Oh, princess, should I say who it's from?" He winked and whisked himself away.

I sat on the stool, eagerly waiting for Teetu to come back. You never knew what Teetu was going to say since he was so bold; he often did the opposite of what I asked or expected, but everything was done in love. I could hear him making his way back; he sang Urdu love poems about the beloved and not being able to separate oneself—and how this feeling of *love* can never be broken.

I started laughing. I couldn't help myself.

"Okay, what happened?" I asked.

"I found him, of course, as I find everyone. It's true: I have never seen such attire on a maharaja. He is a king with much kingship and modesty. I walked up to him and suggested he try my special juice, even though I saw he had just finished a glass. He didn't turn down my offer. 'If it's special, I shall try,' the king said. So, I gave him your freshly poured glass. 'Why is it so special?' he asked me. I winked at him. He thought my wink was odd, so I pretended like something was in my eye, princess."

Teetu started laughing hysterically, wiping away his tears.

"The others watched as he drank it. 'Very beautiful recipe. Thank you,' he said. 'It is special. Maybe later you could bring me another glass?' he asked. He resumed conversing with the men. I nodded and left."

Teetu started snapping his fingers. "It's almost like he knew it was you—with the comment and his look."

"Do you think he knew it was from me?" I asked

inquisitively, seeking reassurance.

"The question is: Do you believe he knew it was from you?"

"Yes. Yes, I do."

"All that matters is what you believe in your heart. You should go now, as dinner will come soon and your mother will wonder where you have been. And now, I must prepare and put my attention here. No more heart games right now."

He went back to the clay oven to perfect his famous naan.

I could hear the low pitches of the sitar accompanying the tabla. That was my calling: dinner would be served shortly.

"Okay, Teetu, I will see you soon."

He yelled over the crackling sounds from the clay oven. "Yes, princess, soon I will see you."

I opened the door knowing this would be my last minute alone until the party was over. I took each step with deliberate meaning and purpose. The first step I centered my breath, the next breath I inhaled love, and the last breath was gratitude for this incredible journey I was to experience. When I looked up, the hallways were empty: everyone must have gathered in the dining area already.

"Arjumand, there you are." My sister appeared. "We are waiting for you. The entertainment has started and soon we shall eat," she proclaimed, grabbing my hand and whisking me away.

The formal dining room was the largest room in the palace. The themes, décor, and ambience changed for every event—it held a rich history with rare antiquities. Countless mirrors reflected sheer beauty. The sun set and reflected rubies and pink sapphires—and a few tints of rare violet.

It was intriguing to watch people from different cultures intertwined in one setting. There were guests from every part of the globe—from Asia to Europe. So many customs, traditions, and attires in one room. I never saw such an array of diverse behaviors.

I saw Diya with her daughter and they smiled at me. She waved her hand, gesturing for me to come over. "It is so lovely to see you again. Sorry we had such a brief time and could not resume our chat."

"Arjumand, this is my daughter."

"A pleasure to meet you." I placed my hands on hers.

"You as well, Arjumand. My mother has spoken so highly of your character and your attire."

"I should be the one to say such things. I'm sorry, but I didn't hear your name."

"I'm Yasmine."

"Of course, Yasmine, a fitting name for a princess."

She laughed and embraced me. I felt a connection to her immediately. "I should hope you will come to my wedding."

"Of course, and I assume you will do the same for me."

"When are you getting married?"

"In five years." I made sure this was spoken in a demure and quiet fashion. "May I get you something to drink?" I could see a tray of pineapple and mango juice going by on a silver tray.

"I shall have the pineapple," Yasmine replied.

"Mango for me," Diya requested.

I passed them the glasses, taking a pineapple juice for myself. "Please excuse me. I will come back later."

"Of course, understandably you have much to do," Yasmine stated. Her mother nodded in agreement.

Rows and rows of famous musicians, such as Jagannath and Janardhan Bhatta, offered elaborate rhythms and vocals. But none compared to the infamous Tansen, who had passed on. Some artists were gifted copious amounts of money for their godly talents of harmony. The pitches and tones of the stringed veena mingled seamlessly in heavenly unison; the soft tones had their own space and could be heard amongst the deeper ones. I was always amazed at how many different instruments existed. Sitars, pakhawaj, and tanpura: the list was endless. I hoped we would dance later. Usually, we did so after dinner.

I saw my father approaching the head of the table. This meant that dinner would be served very soon. He had a grand way of letting guests know when dinner would be served. He would slowly make his way to the head of the table, speaking less and less as he inched toward it.

Oh, and he avoided eye contact. Then he would plant himself in front of his chair, looking down at the ground, waiting for the others to take their designated spots. It was subtly dramatic.

He commanded quite an authoritative presence without even requesting it. And considering who was here and the titles they held, to have them take his cue was very impressive.

What did he have up his sleeve?

I couldn't stop wondering.

What spectacle would he put on?

Before dinner, he always had a dazzling show of some sort. At the last dinner party, he charmed a cobra while he played the flute and danced with it. Word traveled around the globe about his distinctive character. Some kings and nobility were known for expressive and eccentric behaviors, but none were like him. Every breath that he lived was done in love; therefore, it was always unique and a surprise. It came from the unknown. A few moments later, he walked in with his prized parrot, Alibaba.

The feast would begin.

अष्टादशन्

My father was out on a camel ride when he saw Alibaba sitting in a peepal tree. My father stopped dead in his tracks, consumed by Alibaba's grace and his pearly white hair with rings of blue and pink around his neck—and sage green eyes. "He could not take his eyes off of me," my father proclaimed.

"Father, I'm sure you wished he was a lady," I joked.

My father liked things that didn't come easily.

It must be why he adored my mother.

The story goes that my father started to whistle. Alibaba stared at my father, turned his head away, and started to whistle the exact same beats.

Did he really just hear this?

He summoned those around him. They, too, agreed that they heard the sounds. My father decided to create a new song to see how this bird would react. This time, Alibaba stared right into my father's eyes and duplicated every note again, adding a little dance at the end of his branch and fluffing his feathers—dazzling everyone.

This can't be, my father thought.

"Mr. Alibaba, I know you live free and do as you please, but would you like to live with me?" my father asked. "You will always be free to do as you like. The grounds are spectacular and you will have many things to seek for adventure. The others thought I had lost my mind," he told me.

In their very Indian accents, they asked, "Um, sir? Sir? You are speaking to a wild bird. Are you okay? Can we get you some water? It is very hot today, isn't it?"

"I am fine—very, very fine. But not as fine as he. How often is it we come upon a bird with such intelligence and understanding? And, of course, sitting in a banyan tree, which speaks of his wisdom. Why this parrot has chosen this one, from the thousands around, shows what he is," my father noted.

My father then extended his hand out like a branch to mimic the one Alibaba was on. He waited patiently. Alibaba just sat still. I think he was contemplating his future and what he thought of this offer. A little while later, Alibaba propped himself onto my father's forearm, walked backwards onto his shoulder, and remained there until my father reached home atop his camel.

My father thought Alibaba knew where we lived and that was why he chose us, as he believed many things come back to life in other forms. That was how our energy reunited—the circle of life. If it was meant to be, nothing could be stopped or changed. When they approached the gates, he flew off of my father's arm and into the palace courtyard.

My father walked over to the musicians and started to play the tabla; Alibaba started singing and dancing. He picked at the strings of the sitar with his beak. The guests were amazed. Even those who maintained their composure watched with wide eyes. They were fascinated and intrigued. By the end, Alibaba was back on my father's shoulder where he began. The guests applauded and my father gestured to the musicians and Alibaba for credit.

"Time to eat," my father declared. "I've worked up quite the appetite, as I'm sure you have. Not you, Alibaba," he joked.

I wondered what the king thought of my father.

Was he amazed?

Was his father like this?

I wished I could be near him to see his expression. I let my eyes wander. Where could he be sitting? Two marble tables went down vertically all the way to the end of the dining room; one side could easily seat at least 75 people. I looked into the mirrored wall to see if I could find his reflection, as faces were reflected from the candlelight and lanterns.

And there he was.

"Are you okay?" Parwar queried, as she picked up on my frozen state.

"Oh yes, of course, I—"

My father stood to speak "To all who have come, thank you. May the delicacies you are about to devour consume your mind, body, and soul. Happy New Year! May we celebrate together always."

The clinking of glasses accompanied my father's warm wishes. As the guests started to dig into the food, I waited for Teetu to come around.

Come on, Teetu, come on.

I saw he was at the other table, at the opposite end, being complimented on his famous naan. He always came to check on me as soon as he had some free time. I knew it would be very soon. I doused my rice with yellow curry and yogurt. I like to arrange my food like my moods, either abstract or a design specific to my mood—especially in intoxicating moments like this. This one was an abstract heart, which opened with every movement of my fork.

"More pineapple? My famous naan?" Teetu offered.

"Teetu, I've been waiting for you."

"Yes, princess, at times I must serve others besides the most important one."

"Teetu, when you have time, could you please serve the juice again?"

"Yes, Rani. As soon as I am done serving, I will do so." He clinked the bowl and shook his head.

I ripped off a piece of naan and dipped it into my dhal. I closed my eyes and with that one bite, I was taken away. *Teetu, you outdid yourself again*, I thought. The fluffy moistness and the spices of the Orient were perfected by a master's hands.

I ate like an elegant bird since I was situated almost directly across from the king. I made sure my movements were executed with a delicate precision and exoticism—not unlike a peacock. I wasn't an elephant bird that left crumbs or traces all over my face and beak. Parwar gave me odd looks, which I tried to ignore. She never saw me eat in such a refined way.

I learned through watching him that I was correct in thinking that the lady I saw disembark from the elephant with him earlier was the king's wife—along with his mother and father.

Did he love her?

She was beautiful. Even I couldn't take my eyes away from her whimsical beauty. His mother had the same delicate mysterious features, except hers carried a pathway of fine lines from having lived longer. I couldn't see much of his father in him, but I could hear his father from my side of the table speaking in a loud, stern voice. It was direct as he purposefully over-pronounced every word.

The king replied calmly in a tone that was smooth and sensual with deep, rich hints of his soul. I couldn't hear everything he said because his voice rose and fell depending on what he said and what he emphasized. He spoke not to be heard or to command attention like his father—more like his soulful grandfather, Akbar.

Eating this way—with such formalities and displaying such manners—restricted me to eating half the amount I would normally consume. I was starving, so I decided to give up and go back to my typical animal-like ways since this show was far too difficult to produce. And if he didn't like the way I ate, well, obviously we weren't meant to be.

Though I didn't think he would mind.

Perhaps he would even find it endearing.

I heard Teetu across the table talking about the juice. I looked directly at Teetu, which the king saw and picked up on, and gave him a reason to look at me.

He thanked him for the heavenly juice. With his lips pressed against the cup, he stared at me and we locked eyes. I giggled to myself and grabbed my napkin to hide my expression. The perfect cover: dabbing my mouth like a lady. I learned this coy move from the European women I saw around.

The plates were being cleared and the room was being transformed into a temple of sugar. A separate table of scrumptious, invigorating, and mind-changing sugary treats from around the world drew my attention. I never saw such colors and wrappings. If the desserts were anything like the wonderful and unique attire the guests wore, I was surely in for a surprise—as were my taste buds.

But my dream dessert is, was, and always will be gulab jamun, a liquid coconut syrup mixed into a glazed ball that is doused in spices with cinnamon and shredded coconut tops. Topped off with a cup of hand-brewed chai with ginger, cinnamon, and cardamom. That was something I never rejected or turned a blind eye to no matter how hard I tried.

My mouth salivated with the thought of it.

A sugar feast not for the faint of heart.

I heard voices chattering in many languages that I didn't understand, even though I spoke Persian, Arabic, Urdu, Hindi, and Sanskrit. It was said that Sanskrit was the universal language of the gods, the language of the soul. My father knew some English due to his work affairs, and even a small amount of the Oriental languages. My mother paid no mind to languages, as it wasn't one of her interests and there were translators.

I watched as many faces and titles came to greet the king. I heard that Prince Khurram was becoming Shah Jahan. He was ascending to being the throne-bearer after his father, King Jahangir. The preparations had begun.

Akbar was close to the Shah at all times. I noticed how they always found a way to be near each other. Maybe that was why he had more of his grandfather's disposition than his father's.

Birbal was hysterically laughing and making witty jokes from "samasya purti," which is when Akbar gave lines to Birbal and Birbal had to add lines in order to fill the gaps or issue at hand. It was said that many Muslims despised Birbal, for he made Akbar renounce Islam. Akbar even created his own religion called "Din-i-llahi," which Birbal followed. It incorporated all religions as one, from Christianity to Islam Zoroastrianism, Jainism, and Hinduism. In his religion there were no sacred texts, temples, priests, or rituals; the only commandment was to be kind to one another and not eat meat on the month of your birthday. Many citizens condemned his religion, for it held no signs of the typical entrapments like the religions that had been established.

He convened his council for every decision that had deep meaning—even now. He sought to go beyond routine thoughts and patterns to achieve profound life-changing effects and desires for all. He stopped the enforcement of conversion to those with different religious faiths and beliefs——and eliminated the taxation of non-Muslims. These ideologies were imbedded deeply because of old-school rules and patterns that were never challenged or changed until Akbar.

One story that made me love him even more was when he set up a hunt with all of the animals of the jungle—from the ones that could touch the sky to those that could never hide, as well as others that could pass by you in a blink of an eye.

None were to be ignored.

Akbar heard a voice through an animal he killed. The voice told him that animals were of life; they were our guides and spirit-holders. It spoke how animals never hide behind a mask like man, yet man fears them and kills them because of their truth and wildness. Man came from animal, yet he hides his animalistic ways until he acts upon them and kills unnaturally with a weapon. When man and animal lived as one, the universe was in harmony; but when man began to ruin the circle of life, it created chaos and destruction.

One cannot gather God's creations that live in true beauty of instinctual form and take their fates into their hands for pleasure or game. If one keeps killing, all will go in extinct. And then what natural beauty will exist? What makes man think that he is above all and can take life into his hands and choose fate and death? When did God speak to man and tell him that he could take the life of another? What kind of cruel god would create such ways?

He cancelled the hunt right then.

Shortly after, he became a vegetarian.

The panoramic doors to the balcony opened.

"Is dessert desired outside? Come, please join us." My father invited the guests, leading them outside.

I knew I could not, but I wanted to take my dessert to my quarters to observe this spectacle from afar, where I could discreetly take it all in—like a falcon soaring the skies over its prey. The king's parents, King Jahangir and Taj Bibi Bilqis Makani, were engrossed in conversation with my mother and father as they made their way into the gardens.

My father introduced them to his vast variety of exotic marigolds, blue jasmines, and roses. His nose touched the centers of the rosebuds ever so delicately. His beloved trees spoke their names and their stories—from Durga to Sarasvati and Lakshmi (and everything in between). My father's fingers gracefully traced over the trunks and branches. He changed the garden's imagery depending on his emotions, the seasons, and the moon's moods. He told the unspoken stories of his inner world through the garden's creations.

My mind went around in circles as to what could be unfolding. What were they talking about? Was it about me? Should I go over and see? Maybe I should wait until they summoned me? Did the king mention our meeting?

"Arjumand, you're all alone?" the unknown guest queried.

"Oh…no, I have spoken too much. I was just watching the sunset and admiring the night. Just taking a moment. That's all."

"Yes, the grounds are stunning," she said. "Your mother and father are…."

That was all I heard.

I cannot recollect what she talked about for the next twenty minutes, nor her name. I was so caught up in my fantasy that reality ceased to exist. I nodded and gestured to suggest I was politely engaged, while my focus and heart ran elsewhere.

"Arjumand, would you please come down? I need you. Sorry to break your engagement." My father apologized to the guest. "She can resume the conversation when we are done."

I took a deep inhale and made sure my exhales were just as long as I purposefully took my steps. I was careful not to catch the bottom of my skirt on my feet, as the steps were steep and I was barefoot. The marble and sandstone seemed hot despite the night being cooler. As I made my way to the last step before the gardens, my father held his hand out to me. He always did so to guide me.

"Eating to your little heart's content I see."

He whispered so the others couldn't hear.

"Oh yes, baba, you know I cannot resist the sweetness. It just melts in my mouth and takes me away. Up, up, and away. And these new delicacies are otherworldly."

"Oh, Arjumand, everything in your world takes you away——and I hope it will forever. Actually, I know it will. Please come, for there is an introduction that awaits."

एकान्नविंशति

She eyed me as though I was a precious sculpture. "What a beautiful child you have," his mother observed, inspecting me ever so closely. Almost simultaneously, my parents thanked her. "Her face is regal and divine. Her features look like a painting."

I learned through the introduction that her name was Taj Bibi Bilquis Makani. Even though I already knew this, I acted as if this was the first time I heard it. Of course, I had to formally address them with proper titles of *King* and *Queen*, *Shah* and *Shahbanu*, and then their names.

To disclose your real name and full name was a matter of trust, as names have powerful symbolic meanings. They reveal your past identities and path, an entrance into a sacred world.

"What is it that keeps your time?" Shahbanu Taj asked.

"Well," my father spoke, "what doesn't keep Arjumand busy? She is young, but she is educated in the arts, yoga, astronomy, religions, design, and views some of my political affairs and dealings in passing."

The queen was impressed by what she heard. Most practiced simpler and more traditional ways, even when highly versed.

"There are so many things I love to do," I responded with a soft tone. "I love to paint and create, to recite Mathnawis and learn of great Sufi mystics, to study battle and conduct, and to ride elephants. That is just a glimpse into my world. Oh, and I can gaze far too long at jewels." When I spoke those words, I looked right through him.

"You ride elephants?" she asked incredulously. "I would not have anticipated that."

My mother gave me a look that let me know I may have disclosed a bit too much. To talk about everything and anything with little to no thought was a blessing and a curse. After what seemed like a long pause and silence, I grabbed my father's hand in adoration.

"I must have been only five or six when I was playing in the gardens with our elephant, Ganesh. My father saw how I was swinging side to side on her trunk, hoping that I would make my way onto her back—like I saw my father do. But that never happened. Day after day, I tried. All I did was skim the dirt and fly in the air on my dear elephant's trunk. She, too, was confused as to what I was trying to do. After watching all of my measly attempts, my father decided that he would teach me once and for all. He showed me how to lower Ganesh's head, grab the back of her ears, walk up her trunk, and crawl onto her neck."

Silence.

Oh no, I said too much.

His mother finally spoke. "Have you met my son, Arjumand? He, too, loves elephants. I have yet to meet a girl who does as much as he."

I didn't know how to reply to her.

Have I met your son? Yes, in my dreams, in the market, and everywhere in between. He has lived with me in my bedroom all my life—ever since I came to know of him. I painted him in every vision since Kabir spoke of our destiny when I was a child. I just stared at her until I could gather and find the words, as well as to make sure I wasn't disclosing more than what was needed yet again.

"I have seen him in passing today. Unfortunately, I'm sorry to say that is all I can account for. How lovely that he and I share such a fondness for animals."

"My son, Prince Khurram," Jahangir spoke. I could smell faint wine lingering from his breath as I bowed.

The king placed his hands before me in prayer and I placed mine to mimic his. I then bowed and touched his feet.

"The pleasure is mine," he said. I could feel our parents looking at us, not knowing if they felt like these seconds lasted too long or knowing and seeing that what we had was magical. I was sure that my parents knew. I softly and discreetly rubbed my palms against each other, missing the touch of his skin.

"Arjumand was telling us of her love of elephants and I told her of yours. I knew you needed to meet, if you hadn't already," his mother explained.

"Elephants." He stared off into the distance. "You have a love of elephants? That's rare for a Shahzadeh."

I wanted to share and unravel all of my hidden secrets, but knew this was neither the time nor the place. "I am quite fond of gajas (elephants)," I coyly revealed. "I know the strength they hold in great stillness. Their courageous hearts are fiercely loyal and patient."

He listened intently and nodded in acknowledgment before turning to his left and whispering into his mother's ear. A few moments later, he looked into my eyes and spoke. "I must have you."

Silence lingered between us as we walked through the maze.

"You came to find me today, didn't you? How long have you known? When did you know that you were going to ask me to marry you?" The questions tumbled out of my mouth, one after another.

"Shahzadeh, sometimes too many words spoken leave far too little to the imagination. I shall tell you piece by piece when the story serves its time and the moments are right. I will not speak just to speak—to amuse your mind. At times I may answer, but other times I will be myself and do what I please. I shall let you have your freedom to do the same."

I was taken aback.

"Thank you. I don't know how to respond."

He laughed. "I just told you. Words don't always need to express what is unspoken, but known, between us."

As we walked through the grounds, many eyes watched us. I assumed that they heard. The women watched in awe and even from afar, their eyes spoke of a slight jealously for themselves and their daughters.

A marriage arrangement never unfolded this way.

Parents were the ones who chose who you married and formally met to discuss all dealings, sometimes even before a child's birth. If both parties agreed—usually for political agendas, monetary reasons, or family titles—then a formal introduction was arranged and the wedding ceremony was unveiled.

To choose your beloved and love at first sight was unheard of.

My aunt claimed that she just heard the news from my mother and her husband, King Jahangir; she was beside herself with happiness. It was now known, and known all over the world, that I was his. The compliments and flattery came from every direction.

I was formally introduced to his wife, Kandahari Begum, which meant "Lady from Kandahar." He placed his hand in hers to acknowledge her presence and held my hand with the other. "I would like you two to meet, as I have asked for Arjumand's hand in life as well."

She held the most beautiful cat I ever saw with jewels for eyes. "What is your cat's name? I'm very fond of exotic cats."

"Her name is Tara, for she is my little star. I take her with me everywhere. The king knows how fond I am of cats and their wild ways. When you move into the palace, you will be able to meet all of them. I have so many I wouldn't even know how to count. Some appear and disappear, and others never leave."

I smiled.

As I did, I saw flashes of memories from lifetimes ago. I went to touch her hand and kissed her on the cheek. When she kissed me back, her lips faintly slid against mine. I questioned if it was done purposely or if it was an innocent accident. I could smell the amber attar that lingered on her skin. It was known that amber evokes sensual pleasures and ancient wisdom. The king looked at our woven hands that never separated.

"I do look forward to your presence in the palace. I know we will get along lovely," she promised. "There are so many things that I wish to show you. If you need anything, or if I can be of service, please do not hesitate to ask, Arjumand."

I couldn't feel jealously toward her, even if it meant sharing the one who was meant for me.

I, too, fell in love with her.

विंशति

Though my mother and father held a great deal of power and wealth, it was nothing compared to what they were exposed to now. There were many formalities and new political acquirements and acquisitions to which they had to adhere. The king gifted my parents and me with extreme extravagance, which I paid no mind to. He refused my parents' continual gestures of gifts, which wasn't standard protocol. He stated that he didn't desire anything from them, except for one thing—me. However, he always accepted the sweets and presents I gifted him.

The ancient texts said that materialism and wealth have no meaning except for those who live for the earthly plane. I knew that he was born into an empire of exorbitant wealth and I didn't want to allow for that to change who I was or the voices I spoke for. I meditated more and deepened my breath so I could shed my ego and live within, so the illusions and pictures I was going to live in didn't overtake the purity of my soul.

As I laid in bed, I pondered many ideas of what my life would become. It would undoubtedly be a surprise, as I never existed in that world before. I had never experienced it. I was born with such freedom that it raised many eyebrows; and how we lived as a family was rare. My father had only one wife, which was unheard of. Now I would be married to a man who had one wife and could acquire an endless surplus like his father and grandfather. He could even gather "muttas" if he desired, which involved no ceremony but a pact between a man and woman for a limited time.

How would I feel?

What if he didn't have enough time for me? How would he choose who he wanted? Were we to rotate days with him? In which quarters would I sleep? Would we all sleep together in one big bed?

The questions in my head were never-ending, for my imagination was infinite. The deeper I went into meditation, the more sacred scriptures I read; they centered my thoughts. When I connected to my soul I became "maya" and could play with the universe. The stories in the *Bhagavad Gita* stuck to my soul like a second skin as my third eye awoke. My favorite story was about the goddess Parvati and her wild love affair with the untameable, omnipotent blue god, Shiva. Shiva was madly in love with Pavarti and being the god of destruction and creation, his emotions could be quite erratic.

One day, Parvati desired a bath and told her son, the elephant god Ganesh, not to let anyone in. No matter who it may be. Ganesh sat at the door guarding it with his life, declining all who appeared before the door to seek his mother.

"I'm sorry I'm not allowed to let you in," the patient, kind elephant god spoke.

After some time, his father, Shiva, came to the door and demanded to be let in. Ganesh kindly declined his demand.

The elephant god spoke, "I'm sorry, but mother told me that none are to be allowed in, whomever they may be."

Shiva, the god of destruction, became enraged at being told "no" and chopped off Ganesh's head. When Parvati came out and saw Ganesh's severed head and bloody, lifeless body, she was beside herself and begged Shiva to bring her son back to life, for she instructed him not to allow anyone in.

Shiva ran into the jungle, distressed, at the sorrow he inflicted upon his beloved. He pondered life and creation, and how he could produce another child for her from nothing. All of a sudden, a baby elephant appeared. From that he envisioned his son as the compassionate elephant god. He gently cut the elephant's head off and placed it atop his son's body.

I took this message from the Bhagavad Gita, "If you want to see the brave, look to those who can return love for hatred. If you want to see the heroic, look to those who can forgive."

And that was how the wise Ganesh came to be.

Kabir and the mullah (religious master) were atop the towers reciting endless scriptures for protection and longevity that echoed all around the palace from every dome and balcony to where they sat. I was to join them to cite verse after verse of Surahs and ayats.

I tried to keep my focus on the black calligraphy, but everything from the texts became a blur; my imagination was elsewhere. Not to mention the many distracting hands. My scalp was massaged with the richest amla oil and my third eye was opened and sealed with a special elixir Kabir created from agar oil. The rare aphrodisiac of the agar tree was revered and said to be the incense that burned during the sacral burial of Jesus. I closed my eyes and peered in between my eyebrows and saw the universe unfold.

When the mullah left, I broke my silence. "What are you doing now?" I asked. "He's gone. We don't have to assume formalities to appease him and the laws of the gods. You don't have to be a mystic anymore, Kabir. We can now change costumes."

"I am aligning your chakras and working on the last one. The one that is always ignored."

"And which one would that be?"

He placed his icy hands on my feet. "The ultraviolet one, the one of the invisible breath." It felt as though my veins turned violet with the touch of his hands. "Love and bliss exists far past what is known of this universe. It connects you to the earth and heavens—and grounds you from your roots to the constellations up above far past the endless skies. Long before you began, where you lived as a god among the cosmos."

I put my hands over his.

"I hope one day that you, too, shall feel the love you once had."

He chuckled. "To experience pure, unconditional love is rare. My child, when you love, it comes with a form a suffering or dying. One must see the blessing and have gratitude. As I live now, I have come to love all, for that is 'lila,' the divine play of life. The universe was created from freedom and creativity, which began with breath. All that exists lives within your body, for every element of a star exists within you. When you are born, you are nine months old and the body has begun to die. And when the corpse goes, that does not mean that the love that once lived in a body dies or changes from what it was that you have experienced. Love never dies. Energy never dies, even after death. It goes with your soul."

A single tear ran down my left cheek onto my heart. "If that is what comes with true love, so be it. May I, too, experience its depth. That is my *kismet,* Kabir."

एकाविंशति

The time had arrived for the betrothal: January 30th, 1607.

"Arjumand, are you ready?" my mother called.

With each step I took, I spread my toes, picturing ultraviolet light as Kabir painted. As I made my way to the final step, I embraced my mother and father. I wanted to feel them forever. I didn't want to let go. It took a few moments to tear myself away from those who wished to engage in a simple chat, but as I did, I sipped on the most scrumptious chai with ginger.

"Shall we?"

My mother placed her hand out and I placed mine under hers. I learned this in yoga: the dominant hand over the subservient one so the energy could be guided. I desperately needed my mother's grounding energy for this experience.

My father looked like a shah himself in golden pajamas encrusted with gold embroidery and intricate appliqué. My mother and sister wore matching black lehengas with emeralds outlining the elaborate embroidery. Magnificent green gems were encrusted into their jewelled sarpeechs (headdresses) as well, along with adorning finger gems and neck jewels.

Teetu sipped chai by the door. I never saw him dressed so formally. He wore black silk kurta pajamas. It was simple, but for him, very elaborate—no doubt commissioned by my mother

"Maharani, wow. Words cannot say what kind of star you are." He spoke of the stars on my garment. Diamond stars: there were 4,575 of them to be exact. They were identical to the ones I painted on my bedroom ceiling, and they floated off of the royal coat and white silk lehenga.

My mother led me outside, where the elephants were lined up and waiting. My father prepared ten elephants and six camels. That was enough space given that each elephant could host six people while carrying goods. I kissed each of them on their trunks. Decadent howdahs sat atop their backs with murals of ancient tales painted upon them. Those who would be joining had their own modes of transportation.

Normally, the majesty of nature was enough to distract me, but for the entirety of this journey I was consumed with only thoughts of him. I took a few daydreams in between and overheard that we would be at the destination gates in twenty minutes. I opened the curtain of the howdah in excitement and saw a glimpse of a monumental brick wall. There were monkeys sitting along the ledge of the wall. I thought that maybe the king summoned Hanuman and invited them all. The elephants patiently lined up behind one another and walked single file, escorting us through the gates.

It had to be the size of a city.

I turned to my mother in awe. Even Parwar was taken aback. I was worried that she was going to fall out of the howdah; half her body was out, so I held onto her feet just for safety.

We stepped down from the ladder onto the stone platform and walked the rose pathway, which served as a guide and led us to the doors of the marble palace. There were at least five hundred faces behind him from what I could see. I later saw that it was thousands upon thousands in rows that never ended, stretching beyond the deep corridors inside. Those of highest importance were placed closest to the king. My parents greeted his parents and Akbar with a traditional bow, and then with their hands in prayer pose to summon the gods.

I followed suit.

I walked up to the king and faced him. Staring into his eyes, a smile covered the canvas of my face and tears clouded my vision. My feelings were the doors to the eternity inside my soul. When you are consumed by true love, nothing makes logical sense—everything is new, a mystery, a surprise within a surprise.

He bent down to the floor. I didn't know what he was doing; maybe he dropped something. And then I saw that he was picking up the tears of joy I dropped.

Everything inside was cast in white marble, gold, and platinum. The aesthetics were uniquely royal. There were intricate marble benches with hand-painted tales of cities, camel-bone chests carved to appease the ficklest palette, and Jali-latticed screens created with the most breathtaking sacred geometry. The room we gathered in was lit by millions of burning diyas. Diyas were burned to signify the divine while illuminating the universe and the soul.

A pathway of white silk rugs and candles led the way to the enchanting gardens. I walked on his left side and his wife, Kandahari, was on his right.

Nothing mattered except my love for him.

As we sat in the sacred gardens along the serene riverbank, there were many rituals offered to bless the existence of the universe. We spoke the verses of the Quran that sealed our destiny before the mullah (religious guider) and the full moon. When one marries under a full moon, it means the yin energy is as powerful as the yang energy and the union will be blessed.

The king was yet to utter a word.

Even if no words were spoken, I knew what he was saying. We didn't need to speak in order to feel one another. I tried to provoke him by secretly gliding my hands over his bare skin––playing with a little bit of danger.

He remained unprovoked.

He just smiled at me while undressing me with his eyes. I could feel that he wanted to see how dangerous I could be. Touching was prohibited, but that would not stop me.

After what seemed to be hours of saying farewell, the king escorted my family and me to the gates. I respectfully waited for my parents to take their seats first so I could steal a few last moments with him. I quickly grabbed his hand when no one was looking.

I professed my love. "I love you unconditionally forever and you shall see what my love is. You don't have to answer me; you may stay in your state of silence as long as you like."

I turned and made my way atop Ganesh. After a few moments, I opened the curtain and looked at him.

"I know you know that I love you," he whispered.

And with that we were off.

As soon as I left him, I felt like a piece of my heart was missing. I didn't know when I would see him again. It wasn't customary for viewings to take place before the wedding—and that was to be in five excruciating years. The anguish of having to wait left me with a heavy heart.

But as soon as we arrived at the palace, I was given a letter that the king sent. It requested my attendance in the gardens. The king desired my company in order for us to get better acquainted with one another.

My parents agreed.

He arranged for the most breathtaking tea party in the gardens. We rode his collection of prized Arabian horses, read Urdu poetry, and played an array of games—Pachisi and Moksha Patam (snakes and ladders), which was my favourite.

I always won.

Or at least he let me pretend I did. The ladders represented virtues and the snakes were vices. I told him I won by way of virtue in lieu of his vices. We conversed about war and political dealings and agendas. He sought my advice for upcoming battles and asked about my thoughts in regards to the betterment of all.

He widened my eyes to a world I had never experienced or knew existed. He bestowed new universes upon me with thought-provoking questions and rebellious ideas.

We had a wonderful dinner with his wife, Kandahari. The dining room was so beautiful that every time I looked at a piece, it was as if it had suddenly appeared. There was so much for the eye and soul to take in; the room itself transcended one to another dimension and reality. The king had a vision of art and architecture like no other, which I assumed he inherited from Akbar.

Kandahari sat next to me the whole time, touching my skin when the moments permitted. Laughter and giggles filled the room. The king had a way of making you feel like you were the only one in a room even if many others were present.

I tried to buy as much time as I could by slowly eating the scrumptious sugary delights and talking frequently while ordering my umpteenth chai. But after so many teas and treats it was time for me to walk to the gates, where he presented me with a jewelled box. When I opened it, my eyes laid sight upon a magnificent ruby spinel pendant with the words "Noor-e-Jahan."

"I made if for you from a dream, because that's what you are, the light of the universe."

He put the breathtaking necklace on me and I turned to touch his heart. I kissed his cheek and with that I was off.

The following morning, I was questioned about the vision of my creation. The most distinguished tailors from Karkhanas were commissioned. Several thousands had already begun to work on the king's newly commissioned closet for our upcoming vows—silk Jama robes, Patkas for his jewelled swords, regal turbans, and Jhutis designed only for a king's feet. He gifted me the most extravagant jewelled pyjamas to do yoga in. The craftsmanship was so flawless that even a magnifying glass could not find a seam—nor a beginning or an end. How could human hands create such magnificence? It amazed me how only one set of hands could craft such rarity; they were a specialist's specialist, the rarest of the rare.

I symbolically chose to wear a peshwaz, as I was born under the Virgo moon—the September moon of purity and the goddess of harvest. A black bodice of luxurious Jamawar silk from the Orient was what the flowing dress was to be comprised of and it was to be adorned with precious stones and diamonds. It would be finely stitched with zari (gold threads) and endless amounts of transparent muslin, which would appear like fluffy white clouds. When I walked, it would look like rippling ocean waves. The stars were six-pointed Hindu talismans representing Shatkona, the divine masculine and feminine becoming one, which were block-printed upon the silk and finished with minuscule diamonds so that when the light struck, they would illuminate and appear as if they were shooting stars dancing across the sky. I had secretly imbedded symbols of my life that held great meaning for me. The powers of the sky revealed my destiny as Kabir predicted.

My mother designed an assortment of jewels and commissioned them: chunky jadau jewels; hippo thumb rings; polki diamonds made into a jungle of masterpieces; jewelled sandals that roped all the way up the calf—with matching nose rings and ruby sarpeechs. I loved the arsi mirrors because you could admire yourself and your beloved in the reflections. Some of the rings were so large that they covered three fingers and encircled my wrist with a diamond bangle. Brilliant centerpieces were inlaid inside, bustling around riverbeds of jewels. You couldn't look away from the blinding gems, even if you tried to. They were the rarest cuts, carats, and colors, with the most sought-after treasured talismans.

My favorite was a set of cat earrings with a matching emerald cat pendent: "tears of the moon," forest emeralds for eyes, and whiskers of black sapphires. Emeralds were known to channel love through the heart chakra and bestow wisdom and domestic bliss. Cats were highly revered, for they surrender to God and the unknown. They live a cosmically appointed life of deep meaning that they have earned from their previous incarnations. Ancient fables and tales spoke of them as gatekeepers and magic-holders of special djinns.

During this time, Parwar secured a husband, a sheikh named Farid, who was the son of Nawab Qutubuddin Koka. My father knew his father quite well; he was the governor of Badaun. He also happened to be Shah Jahan's father's foster brother. She had a beautiful engagement and wedding. Parwar immediately moved out of the palace, as her astrological forecast permitted her to do so.

द्वाविंशति

My bedroom was like walking through heavenly gardens: there were vases everywhere filled with sunflowers, violets, cockscombs, and every flower you could imagine. Otherworldly fragrances filled my senses; each breath was so different because the prana (energy) was so divine.

When a beautiful white dove appeared at my window, it was like a dream within a dream. I always kissed the doves on their foreheads before they presented his gifts, as I knew they were the messenger between us. I would stroke their feathers and I could still feel the warmth of his touch. I never knew what story he would bestow upon me or where I would be taken to. He wrote on the most delicate stationery about how the universe contrives a plan for lovers to come together, no matter what earthly battle they endured. Somehow, he always felt like he was by my side. Or maybe that was God.

My beloved Arjumand,

One may walk blindly all his life thinking that his eyes have seen and known. But the eyes have no meaning if they only see that of the earthly realm. Unless they have loved, they will be blind, even if one has sight. The eyes must become a vision of the soul that has wandered and walked away from the world into the ethereal towards the gods.

I then asked: Where is this? Where can it exist?

Who beholds this rare gift, when one reaches above the stars and lives with the gods?

And the voice whispered your name in my ear: "You are the entirety of the universe, the infinity of all."

When I look into your eyes, I see all that I was, all that I am, and all that I am to become. So, there is no more need to search or to find a door to knock upon to find the answers.

Nothing is needed, except for this godly elixir that only you possess, which has the name love, "Kama," from the soul of the gods in Sanskrit.

Your Beloved from Every Destiny

The king arranged for the manjha ceremony to take place at his magnificent palace in Jaipur on Mansagar Lake. Rajasthan was known as the King's world, "Raja" king, or "Sthan" place. We were to journey there by elephant and camel. The staff had set forth many preparations that were needed for the long course.

We leisurely began by walking through a forest, stopping to watch the majesty of wildlife. My eyes laid sight upon sloth bears and water buffalos. I wished to see an exotic animal, such as a leopard or an Asiatic lion. We had a light meal atop the elephants by a beautiful water bank, which I swam in with Ganesh, surrounded by lush greenery. When we finished, we were on our way again, trekking through the rich jungle. We slept in luxurious tents and stargazed deeply into the night.

Some days later, we entered my favorite (and last)

destination atop camels: the barren lands of the Thar Desert. I looked around bewildered by the sand dunes and intense heat that threw flecks of golden sand into the air. Even though nothing existed in the land, something holy lived here. Every sacred text has spoken so.

The desert gypsies wore beautiful ornate silver jewellery and the most colorful ensembles. They joyously danced while charming snakes to ancient myths. Their skin was like gold reflecting diamonds from the luminous desert sun. Their eyes carried an extraordinary presence, which they may have achieved from sun-gazing. Gazing at the sun during early sunrise and sunset with your bare feet in the natural earth was known to bring paranormal powers and heal the body.

When my eyes set sight upon the water palace, I felt like I was hallucinating. How could it be that a marble palace floated upon water in the middle of the desert? As hands guided us off the wooden rafts, the first sensation that I felt was warm marble heating my feet from the desert air.

While no one frequented the sandstone and marble palace, except for picnics and duck hunts, it remained lavishly furnished inside with ornate architecture and endless murals— —along with a great many servants. Only one floor was visible; four floors were submerged beneath the waters.

How did water not seep inside?

It was haunting. When I went below, I felt as though I, too, was a part of the underworld. It was another world. One I never knew could exist.

My mother commissioned golden lehengas for all of us to wear. The rich silk felt like melting butter on my skin against the desert heat. I dipped my hands into the clay pot filled with golden turmeric and proceeded to chase the girls and throw it upon them. They scurried around in their yellow garments and tried to gather as much turmeric as they could. The balconies were so slippery and grand that I slid from one side of the palace to another as I chased them or tried to make an escape. There were turmeric stains everywhere—on the walls, all over the floors, on his precious art, and all over us.

My mother playfully doused me in a thin veil, an offering of eternal bliss and happiness. Turmeric was used during these ceremonies because it was highly regarded for fertility, prosperity, and luck—as well as the worship of Surya, the sun. I wasn't to bathe and had to stay coated in the yellow powder; it was a wedding custom.

I ate so many sweets and decadent dishes that I was grateful the garments I brought along had so many ties and elastics that I could easily loosen. Even though there were countless bedrooms and I had a designated quarter, I slept with my mother.

I adored being next to her.

For two days, we played luxuriously and joyfully. Beauty rituals, secrets, and dreams were shared as we lounged in our cashmere blankets. We fell asleep inhaling the intoxicating jasmine and hyacinths from the gardens.

As we set foot to leave, my mother presented us with beautiful customized wooden boxes with a personalized gold belt, carved and painted to our body's perfection. Some of the belts had detailed faces of kings and queens, while others were intricate floral designs. I promised the walls of the palace that when the king and I were married, we would come and create our own memories. I looked back at the palace with a rush of beautiful emotions as I sat atop Ganesh.

When we arrived at the palace, it was time for the mehendi ceremony. My mother had all of the water fountains and basins of the palace filled with her and my aunt's precious rose-oil attars. All I could smell was the exquisite fragrance. Parwar and I playfully doused each other in rose petals as the elders recalled their youthful memories in delight.

I was covered in not only turmeric, but roses.

"Shall we?" my mother sang as she led us to a secret location up the pathway to a door of purple Jamawar curtains. The trees trunks were wrapped in regal velvets; candles floated in glass water bowls, creating a feeling of euphoric bliss and serenity in the gardens. The marble tables were covered in the loveliest jewelled mosaic silk covers, boasting over a hundred recipes of decadent aromatic dishes with rare spices sprinkled atop. There were freshly picked fruits and nuts, pickled treats, and tasty garden delights. There were all kinds of kingly comforts, like luxurious daybeds and hammocks tied between the trees if you wanted a nap. The stacked gifts became almost as tall as the trees, as each and every guest brought a minimum of three—and as many as twenty. It would take forever to unwrap them now. I would save them for later when I was alone.

My mother orchestrated quite the spectacle of entertainment: snake-chanters with mystical flutes, tarot card readings from the divine, and heavenly spoken fables that put you into a dream. Beautiful sutras and the sound of the sitar lingered in the background at all times. The artisans who dipped my toes and fingertips in the blood-red henna painted sacred suns on my inner palms that spoke to me through the karmic forces of the mehndi plant's magical powers.

We smoked mango-flavored beedi with opium, which got me a little light-headed. Even the elders partook in a few smoke halos, which hypnotized them. It was endearing to see many of them fall asleep upon the fluffy pillows on the floor whilst getting their mehndi done. Even though they had bedrooms in the palace, they didn't want to miss out on such a sight—or at the very least to hear of it.

I didn't sleep much, perhaps a few winks before I awoke. But I felt balanced and serene. I took my lukewarm, half-finished cup of chai with me as I made my way through the gardens. I looked at the flowers and their blossoming ways—how they grew, how some died, and how something new was always birthed from death.

Stillness birthed life. Silence breathed life.

As a child, I remembered how I thought nothing changed and nothing died. How innocent my mind was to believe such thoughts. Maybe I was lucky that I saw life that way. But as life evolved, I came to understand that everything is a series of moments simultaneously and seamlessly put together, and written by the author up above.

"Arjumand, please don't be too long. Kabir is on his way." Those were the first words I heard from my mother as I entered the palace doors.

"Yes, mother, I will come down once I have freshened up."

"Please do so."

My bath had been drawn for me. It was the perfect temperature—not too hot and not too cold. I missed soaking my body in water; my body missed its purity. Seeing as how I was not allowed to bathe for days and was covered in turmeric and petals, the water quickly changed its essence.

I looked out the window as my mind wandered. The city was cast in black with hints of gold. I loved to watch the world unfold from my window while hidden in my bath, watching its undertakings and its many preparations—the many lives that unfolded. And now, in the quietest hours, invisible creatures were heard. The tranquil gardens barely breathed and their petals were closed. My animals were in a deep meditation; so much so, that they didn't move. One might assume they were sleeping, but they were not.

I wrapped my wet hair into a bun, grabbed a shawl, and quickly descended down the staircase. My mother was in the library having a discussion with my father when I walked in. I missed my father dearly even though it was only a few days. I immediately kissed him on the cheek and hugged him, not wanting to let go as he kissed me on my third eye.

"I can see my tiger has missed me, but not as much as I have missed you. I heard my princess thoroughly enjoyed herself," my father said.

"Actually, to quote you: You were ecstatic in divine bliss. What more could my Arjumand ask for than to play in a palace upon the water? Who else could say such words, father? More so, who could even find words that mirror the experiences I've had without being there? Only you."

I took a bite of his mango and lemon bar and quickly ran to the roof to find Kabir and the mullah sitting with their eyes closed, chanting mystical hymns. How they knew I arrived even when I tip-toed there to surprise them, as well as how they simultaneously opened their eyes, I will never know. But Kabir said his eyes could always see, even when they were closed, for the inner eye was always open.

I bowed to their feet and pressed my lips in gratitude against the cold stone floor. They placed their hands on my head one after the other. We sat before each other in a circle, in lotus pose, with the disappearing moon in between us.

"May Allah bless all that is and what is to become of you. Oh Allah, bless, sanctify, and grant peace to those who follow prophet Muhammad and what his disciples are here and blessed to do—which is to love. May we know the true meaning of life, which is to love and seek the divine for all around."

Verse after verse, story after story, all were blessed.

As I laid on the floor in corpse pose, staring at the fading stars, he performed the traditional rituals and rights to appease

Muhammad. I went into such a deep state of meditation that all I could do was sink deeper and deeper into the floor while I listened to his hypnotizing chants.

When I stretched my legs out like a cat, I found Kabir in the same position as when we started—sitting in lotus pose. The mullah had vanished. There was no trace of him except for a black string with a Taweez amulet that he left for me to wear to ward off evil eyes. Kabir sat inside an eye he created made of turquoise, quartz, canvasite, and apophyllite crystals. He stepped out of the center of the eye and guided me inside.

"Sit inside the eye, the I, Arjumand."

The energy was so intoxicating that it sent lightning bolts down my spine; it felt as though I was floating outside of my body, like the time I laid eyes upon the Shah at the bazaar. My third eye pulsed with vibrant colors, geometric shapes, and intricate patterns.

I levitated while I mediated.

This wasn't unheard of in this context. Many can do so, if their frequencies and channels are high enough. They can leave their bodies whenever they chose—in and out of trances, other bodies, different planets, through space and time, and into another's thoughts when connected to the divine.

Kabir walked around the eye with amber and opium incenses, as well as a variety of agar and bodi tree blends, channeled and programmed to call upon the gods—from Kali to Durga. Each god had a scent that would lure them. Sarasvati showed me the finest images of creation, while Kali showed the warrior within, always embracing the spirit's battle when fighting for truth.

I opened my eyes spontaneously and saw a star shower. Stars of all colors—indigo, silver, gold, and white—shot across the sky, leaving their cosmic markings and taking their predestined places.

It was very rare to see a star shower. The gods only showed this phenomenon to those who satisfied their insatiable appetites for love and beauty. As such it was unusual, for such thirst was quite unquenchable.

The morning rituals began in the towers with Majid. I could hear the Sufi masters from my bedroom. The whole palace silently vibrated. You could hear the silent Os in the Oms from all around, but they originated from the sacred southeast direction.

I turned around and found my father watching me. "Your mother said I should wake my angel. However, when I arrived, I saw you and I could not stop staring at such beauty. The words were taken away, Arjumand. I have no words," my father confessed. "The gods have taken them, for they created such beauty when they made you that even divine words cannot compare to your silent beauty."

Tears streamed down my cheeks as I gazed into his eyes. He lifted his hand to catch his tears, which I caught for him. I could feel all of his emotions from a single teardrop.

We ate in silence looking deeply into each other's eyes.

"Good morning, my love. Did you even sleep?" My mother urgently stormed into the bedroom singing her words.

"Yes, I did, mother—luckily. And you?"

"It seems not. Oh, there was far too much to do and to prepare, even though we started ages ago. Maybe the excitement of it all has also kept me up," she revealed. "Your father said that even in my sleep, I am always talking to you. The sun will fully appear soon and we must disembark. Everyone will be ready in the next few hours."

I soaked in a decadent attar bath that my father prepared for me. My father gifted me with 63 magical oil attars in the most beautifully carved crystal itardan bottles—which included jasmine, scents of hina, sandalwood, amber, chameli, motia, and a special suhag blend that would seduce the king and me forever through its notes.

"I will send for the dressers. I can't wait for you to see what I have."

"How does it look, mother? Is it as beautiful as I envisioned in my dreams?" I sat on my bed, eager with anticipation. I watched as many faces and bodies left my bedroom, some slowly and some quickly.

"Go on, go ahead," my mother urged.

Walking up to the veiled gift, I put both of my hands on the edges of the silk to gently pull it off. I gasped, losing my breath. "I can't believe this. How did you come up with this? It is more than I have asked for or what I could dream of."

There were millions of gems, precious diamonds, and jewels stitched into the midnight silk peshwaz. The king was depicted as the ruler of the earth, a sea goat, which aligned with his Capricorn birthday. I was the Virgo goddess from up above, who came down to be with him in rose-gold diamonds.

I was left in the quarters with twenty main helpers, who took hours to dress me and paint the canvas of my face. It felt like forever as they tucked and cinched all of the ties and closures. I wasn't permitted to see myself until the very end— when the last detail was completed. I didn't think my arms were long enough for all of the rubies, sapphires, and diamond bangles they layered upon me. They kept looking for skin that could be adorned and spaces where they could add more jewels from the trunks of jewels the king presented.

"No more please. I beg of you. This is far too heavy."

My eyes were lined with kajal; rose powder flushed my cheeks. I sat as still as I could while the last details were being finished. "Close your eyes, Arjumand."

My long raven locks were separated and braided into two silk plaits and dusted with gold flecks—and then wrapped into a crown. I opened my eyes to see gold dust floating in the air. A vision I held onto dearly for our journey to the king's palace in the desert. I turned to the mirror and slowly walked up to it, trying not to touch the mirror in disbelief.

"Thank you…thank you so much." I went to each and every one of the helpers and kissed them on the cheeks. I locked eyes with each in deep gratitude.

My aunt strolled in regally. "You look beautiful, like a whimsical tale. The guests are ready to descend. Shall we?"

She looked beautiful. My aunt always had an air to her. And how could she not? Being one of Jahangir's many wives, questionably the most influential, made her one of the richest queens to walk India's dirt. Maybe that was why it came to be that Jahangir had her face stamped on a Mughal coin—the first and only woman to be given such a powerful political rank in currency.

"We shall indeed."

I peered through the Jali screen and saw the back of my mother's mane blowing in the breeze. I didn't know where to look: at her breathtaking presence in the pearl-white beaded salwar kameez or at her hand that gestured for me to look at the elaborate howdah she created, which was placed upon my beloved Ganesh's back. Ganesh kept turning her head to sneak a glimpse in admiration; she even tried to peek at herself in the miniscule arsi mirrors adorned upon her.

The excitement couldn't be tamed. The drums began and the musicians in the court started to play the enchanting sounds of ragas. Each raga was specific to inducing a mood, tone, and color. This one was summoning the gods of love.

I stood by Ganesh, petting her trunk.

"After you," my mother said.

Ganesh lowered her trunk to the floor. I sat on her trunk, which acted as a ledge. She curved her trunk and wrapped me in it, and then placed me at the entry of the howdah.

"Just this one day, Arjumand, I thought you would have taken the ladder," my mother said. "But no. Why would I expect such formalities?"

"Why would you ever want me to be ordinary when I was born to be extraordinary?" I positioned myself in between my mother and father, and took their hands. My mother put hers over mine and my father intertwined his. The interior was intimately detailed with many of my favorite things: Sufi poetry, decadent loose teas, silk pillows and throws, floral fragrances made from oud oil, and exotic fresh fruit platters.

We were a short distance from the city, perhaps a few hours. I peeked out of the curtains and looked behind us: there were tens of thousands in our party. Many more joined along the way. I tried to take in as many faces and pictures as I could, but there were far too many.

Instinctively, I could feel Ganesh slowing down as we inched near the gates. The golden gates were the entrance to the kingdom Akbar had created through his legacy for his favorite grandson. He unfortunately passed on a few years before. The king's side of the family was here, as it was tradition for them to appear before us. We approached the entry to the gates, but were recognized long before (and from afar).

The doors swiftly opened.

Iridescent jewel shavings were sprinkled along the path, replacing the dirt roads. The white walls and corridors of every mosque and temple were painted in elaborate murals of mythical love and beauty. The vibrant colors and intricate details left little to my imagination; there was nothing that I would add. I walked through our love story atop my beloved Ganesh.

I noticed that when the animals took a step, a golden footprint was left behind. Footprints of all sizes and shapes left a memory in the glimmering dust. I wondered which feet belonged to the king. I looked around at the thousands of prints, seeing if I could find his.

We were led through a tunnel before separating and dividing at the end: the women turned to the left (the west) and the men to the right (the east).

"Where are we?" I whispered to my mother.

I assumed Akbar created it this way, for he wanted to construct a surprise within a surprise. He loved surprises—especially when he could surprise himself.

I silently thanked him.

A guard opened a black barrier. I could see the light from the sun once again, as well as paradisiacal gardens along the water-banks. The water in the fountains and canals reflected everything. Even the birds that flew up above chirped admiringly as they watched their reflections in the water's mirror. The green hedges in the middle acted as a barrier to keep the women and men apart during the segregated ceremony. The trees were so old that all of their trunk legs interconnected and you could feel their messages through your feet.

I walked on decadent and magical Persian rugs—rugs of intricate perfection. It was known that a hidden flaw was sewn in underneath—unseen. This was the true meaning of perfection: purposely placing a flaw into the illusion of perfection. I stared at the powerful women who sat upon magnificent, illustrious carpets by my side.

We were read verses from the Quran for hours on end by the Maulvi about Muhammad's views on marriage and the afterlife. The Quran spoke of true love being linked to the mystical gardens and the afterlife. We recited the mutual agreement of the Ijab-o-Qubul and the Nikaah-Nama was signed and officiated by the Maulvi. Our fathers acted as the Walids.

The barrier of hedges was removed and I nonchalantly pretended that my cloak fell to the floor. It was a bold move if I say so myself. I didn't need to look up to know that all the women's eyes were on me. I could feel the intense energies. But nothing was as profound as his eyes. He locked eyes with me through the mirror and didn't let go. I could feel his hands undressing me, though it was only his eyes that possessed me. It was erotic and intimate, primal and animalistic.

On this day, I not only became one with my beloved, but a warrior of love for India's people and Mother Nature's land––and all of the animals that graced it. Divinity and human prosperity was what the Mughal Empire was built upon, and what Akbar "The Great" passed down. It would be the legacy that I would carry on.

त्रयोविंशति

The stars dazzled as the night began. King Jahangir assembled his entourage. Guests floated about, sorting their departure details whilst mingling and entertaining themselves however they chose. All of the presents quickly disappeared from atop the backs of the powerful oxen and elephants.

"Why do you love me?" I asked him gently. "Why me?" A calm silence filled the air. "Many could be next to you on such a throne, but you have chosen me. May I ask why?"

"My queen may always ask why, but it is a concern if she doesn't know by now. A queen is not born a queen just because of a title she bears or inherited political prestige. A queen is born this way in spirit—before she takes birth. The gods have infused her with goddess powers that no other can possess but her. One may try, one may seek, or one may order to conquer, but none other shall possess it…unless it is gifted by the hands of the gods. Its rarity is beyond purchase or bargain. How can I, even as a king, demand such things from the gods unless they wish to bestow such a destiny upon me? So, I ask you, where could I find such wonders if it were not in you?"

I inched my toes closer to his so that our roots touched and connected. I felt a familiar set of hands on my back: it was my mother and father. My father kissed my cheek. I put my hand on his cheek and softly looked into his eyes. It was a moment of sadness, joy, and glory—like life and death all wrapped up in one.

"My dear child, our love child sent from the gods." He leaned closer and whispered things that I will never share, for they are far too special to share with anyone else's ears but mine.

As soon as the mystifying music sounded, King Jahangir's elephants took their first step. Brilliant fireworks went off simultaneously. I quickly drew the curtains shut. As soon as my fingers left the fabric, they were immediately upon him.

I faintly pressed my lips against the king's lips, waiting for him to kiss me. He didn't. I didn't even know what to do. So, I wrapped my hands around the nape of his neck and kissed him. I didn't plan for this. I thought I could wait for him to kiss me, so I would know what to do, but I could not bear one minute more. I didn't know what to express, except love—to show him my undying love. The king bit my neck playfully and ran his hands through my endless mane. I could tell he had far more experience than me, but I knew that he felt my passion. There was a familiarity, even though our lips never touched before—except for the words that swam off our lips and met in the air. His hands moved over my breasts and I placed my hand upon his heart. I kept my eyes open as long as I could; however, they won the battle and I fell asleep.

When I opened them again, I saw we arrived at King Jahangir's palace: Jahangir Mahal, the distinguished secret palace in Orchha (which meant hidden). Located in Madhya Pradesh, it sat along two magical rivers—the Betwa and the Jamni. The palace was a mysterious mixture of Islamic motifs and Rajput designs. Many called it one of the finest pieces of architecture built during the Bundela (one who offered blood) dynasty.

We were lined in a row before the chain of justice: gold bells held by two elephants and placed at the entry for those who needed the king's wisdom. On this occasion, the bells didn't stop ringing. For as soon as one entered, another was waiting.

Fifty thousand guests were invited, which would be nothing for the enormity of King Jahangir's palace. It could easily seat and entertain three times that amount, for it was a palace within a palace with separate apartments and towers. It was gifted to the Shah's father by Bir Singh Deo as a symbol of their friendship after one encounter. The north tower was re-gifted to Bir Singh Deo.

An exquisite turquoise-tiled entry opened to the east for protection; symbiotically cut mihrabs faced Mecca. Rich red sandstone and marble with Parchin Kari and precious stones were everywhere. The palace was fitted with regal floating balconies and latticed Jali screens. Mythical animals were carved into the lavish marble staircase. You could stare at the wonders of the world through all of the open archways and domes.

There were many tunnels. Some were secret and led to an assortment of hidden rooms. It was eight levels and each floor and room had a specific purpose. The third floor was where the king met with his subjects.

Jahangir's palace was highly regarded, but it was said to be nothing compared to the Queen of Orchha's temple across the way. Dedicated to Lord Rama, the avatar of Vishnu, with four arms. The temple had a trillion different golden lotuses inscribed into every centimeter of the carved marble, each said to be crafted by a different artisan.

Mughalini dishes of exotic vegetables, curries, dhals, yogurts, and decadent meats arrived and disappeared as quickly as they appeared; they were created by over four hundred cooks. The hakim (royal physician) made sure that elements of medicinal needs were highly incorporated. Each grain of rice was coated in silver to not only aid digestion, but to act as a subtle aphrodisiac. There was qeema matar, Mughlai paratha (made with peppers and meat), keema, kebabs, and pasanda— a well-known meat dish and a favorite of the emperor's. There was also nargisi kofta, murg chaap, and rogan josh made of exquisite lamb.

Many ate meat, but I never acquired a taste for it. It saddened my palate to touch anything that bled and had a heart. I have always believed that no being has a right to take life. It wasn't natural. The expiration of life was in the hands of God, not man.

Meera opened my palm and placed a note in it. I discreetly opened it underneath the table. It said: *I know you know.*

Dessert would be served soon with an assortment of heavenly loose teas. There was shahi turka (the most scrumptious bread pudding made of dried fruits and topped with cardamom), anjeer halwa figs, kesari firni (a rice dish sweetened with saffron), kheer, and ice cream kulfi that made me salivate. The cold desserts even had ice from the Himalayas. Many simply sampled these transcendent delights just for taste.

I believe they were watching their waistlines.

There was plenty of small talk, though my aunt did seem to use some of the time to strengthen her and Jahangir's political positioning with powerful women as she sipped wine in her jade cup. I smiled and nodded my head in simple banter, waiting for the moment when the barrier would be lifted.

"Tea will be lovely. Lavender and mint tea."

I played with the leaves in my cup, wondering if there was a hidden message. There must have been. For as soon as that thought ran through my mind, King Jahangir had the barriers removed. I looked up from my teacup and gracefully walked over to greet the king. I placed my hands in prayer position and bowed, placing my lips upon his feet. I didn't have to bow to him in such a way, but he had a magnetic force that pulled me. Jahangir continued to entertain everyone as he indulged in his ongoing love of opium with his foreign guests. It was a rare treat they could only acquire in exotic India.

"Excuse me for a moment. I shall be back."

I excused myself and walked up the sprawling jungle-faced marble staircase to the second floor of the palace. Of course, there were many powder rooms on the main level, but I wanted a few moments alone. When I found the bathroom I desired, I turned to close the door. He pushed me inside with a finger to my lips and silently closed the door.

"Did you think I was going to let you get far?"

He placed his hands on my hips, searching for the mehendi on my bare skin, discovering my body once again. "I see that you have put all of your animal's names on your body. I, too, am your animal; therefore, I must be on here somewhere. Am I not one of your beloved animals?" he declared as he bit my neck. He explored my body obsessively and intimately in those precious stolen moments. I closed my eyes and pulled him into me as he bent before me. Beads of sweat trickled down the crevice of my breasts onto my stomach. I silently moaned in ecstasy as fluids dripped down my legs.

When I opened my eyes, he was gone.

I tucked the stray hairs that fell out of place during our seductive play and dabbed my lips with a berry stain from a quartz koli.

चतुर्विंशति

Jahangir had twelve plots in the gardens transformed into the magnificent tales from *The Book of a Thousand Tales* by Hezar Afsaneh. Oh, it was utterly magical. The moon and the stars and its ever-transforming canvas were our backdrop. I wore a magical, flowing Mughal gown I designed with the faces of every king and queen of India in precious gems. There were luxurious tents embossed with delicate calligraphy that told tales. You could walk into the world of "The Ebony horse," "Aladdin and Sinbad," or "The Sailor" to name a few.

Magic shows, Ganjifa card games, classical dances, and musical sounds filled every corner. Women adorned in the finest threads from Jahangir's harem danced to classical sounds. The eroticism and seduction from their half-draped bodies captivated everyone. The women from overseas took a liking to the exotic tones from the faraway lands. They swayed their bodies with the dancers to the seductive tones.

My favorite ghazal came on. Music of pure love and ecstasy that intoxicated my soul. How could we not dance? Ghazals last forever, for time ceased to exist in poetic mastery—no beginning and no end.

Just like love.

I pulled him close to me and led him out of the tent of puppetry that overflowed with bodies, weaving ourselves in and out of guests as we found our way to privacy. I pressed my body against his and let our breath do the talking in the gardens. I could read his feelings by his heartbeat, by its rhythm and speed.

I spread my toes into the rich dirt, playfully biting his bottom lip, kissing him softly as we danced under the moonlight.

"I have something to show you," said the king.

I followed him to a secret location.

He took me into the palace and down a narrow corridor to where he opened a door. Two thousand diyas illuminated the grandiosity of the marble Hammam room. There were shadows of golden tigers and panther faces in every form, from paintings to statues.

He undressed me and I stood naked before him. He had a way of not even touching me, but still making love to me. We sat for hours in the bath as he sponged my body and massaged my scalp. We spoke at length; no topic was left untouched. I continued to test fate to see if my naked body could seduce him and lure him into desiring me now instead of making me wait. I wanted him so badly, to feel what it would be like when our souls and skin became one. Even in stillness, it was highly erotic. But once the king had a vision, he knew how it would be and how he would want me; and there was nothing that would change his mind.

Not even me.

पञ्चविंशति

When we arrived at the palace a flock of doves swooped in, putting on an elaborate display in the sky. I looked at my feathered friends and wondered which ones were the bearer of gifts, gathering clues from their markings and eyes. But there were far too many— far more than what visited me. There were spotted doves, laughing doves, emerald doves, and red turtle doves.

"How many do you have? I have never seen so many." I watched the fanciful feathers in awe as they glided through the skies.

"Would you like a story, princess?"

I looked at him and nodded.

"I want all of your stories...forever."

"One day when Akbar and Birbal were strolling through the gardens, Akbar curiously questioned how many doves there were. Birbal adamantly, and hastily, replied that there were 95,463 doves in the kingdom. Amazed by such a reply, Akbar asked: And what if there are more? Again, without hesitation or thought, Birbal replied: My dear king, if there are more doves than what I say, then some have come as visitors. 'And if there is less?' Then I must reply that some have gone on holidays or to other palaces. He laughed. So, my dear queen, that is how many doves reside at our palace."

I watched as their wings opened and expanded to gain their desired position and speed. The emerald doves sparkled like their names, while the spotted doves flew high in the sky. As we crossed the bridge, all 95,463 acted as our chaperones. They careened above the water, leaving breathtaking reflections of their silhouettes.

Instead of stopping at the jewelled palace doors, the elephant was guided to the left through a dense forest on the outskirts of the main kingdom.

"Where are we going?" I asked.

"I have a surprise for you."

"What kind of a surprise could you have for me?"

"Close your eyes and you will see." Even though it was mere moments, I eagerly waited in anticipation. "Please open your eyes."

Before my eyes was a majestic white marble elephant's head with a sprawling jewelled trunk that came down to act as stairs with enormous ears for balconies. The face was executed with such precision that every fine and minuscule detail, down to the tusks, was etched to perfect mastery.

"Oh, please, do take me into the wise one's world."

We walked up the marble trunk hand in hand. I couldn't help but to jump a few of the steps in excitement of what was ahead. There was a marble pool filled with glistening rose petals where I dipped my toes, watching as the peacocks admired their reflections.

"My queen, one night I had a dream that I must explain. Come in. Please let me tell you."

Two steel doors opened.

"Would you like some tea? I have waited far too long to share this dream with you. One night after you visited, I laid in bed staring at the ceiling, wondering how long it would be until you would be with me, next to me, indefinitely. As my eyes drifted away in meditation, a vision appeared. It was you atop a white elephant. I saw you *flying*. White elephants, as you know, are the karmic creations of higher beings. Elephants first appeared to Indra during the turning of the waters to produce a milky ocean. And Buddha was conceived through an omnipotent dream, where his mother envisioned him as a white elephant. It was spoken to me that you were to be called Mumtaz Mahal—the chosen jewel of the palace. For that is what you are: a jewel from the gods."

I followed his eyes to gaze upon the ceiling, which held a mural of flying elephants; one was even depicted as me. The magnificence of the artistry was surreal. A Bengal eagle owl swooped in and perched on the helper's forearm and stared at me. Orange eyes pierced through me: I never saw such fluorescent eyes, except in my imagination. The coloring and markings were like a Bengal tiger. I positioned my arm like a perch as well, but he decided to prop himself on my shoulder. I could feel his sharp nails as they dug into my skin. It was known that owls possessed the wisdom to enter one's soul.

"I know you have wanted one for a long time. Of course, he wants to get close to you. Then again, who does not? I must pay mind to these collections of love I accumulate for you. For I see that there may be a battle for your attention."

He grabbed my hand and led me down the corridor that was lined with burning diyas on the floor. At the end of the hall there was a dramatic black door. He placed his hand on the knob.

"I don't know if my masterpiece is worthy of your praise. But your eyes will tell all."

He opened the door and gestured for me to enter. It was pitch black except for the incandescent candles that reflected all of the Mughal mirrors, which covered an entire wall. There was an antique Chinese chest with far too many drawers of all shapes and sizes; who knew what apothecary and magic potions it held. The incenses and fragrances were ambrosial––rose and jasmine lingered throughout, an aphrodisiac of its own. My feet felt as though I was walking upon clouds as they sunk into the exotic embroidered carpets. The canopy bed was exquisite with a beautiful backdrop of hand-painted leather and the most luxurious silk throws and sheets that melted into my fingers.

"Do you like it? I'm sure you know why I have chosen each and every item you love. I have created this creation as a sacred place for our love."

I looked at him and didn't speak, but as he said, my eyes did. I watched as he walked around the room. I could always see his animalistic ways in his walk. I followed behind him as he led me to the wall of mirrors. Our faces and bodies became uncountable in the reflections. It reflected every face we had lived together. I could tell by his eyes that he wanted me to undress. Or maybe I was offering myself as a goddess to a god. I wanted him so badly; I had waited far too long. Piece by piece, all of the jewels and garments fell to the floor. I pressed my breasts against his chest and traced my nails down his back. Tantra tells of how the fingers induce sensuality through a soft touch. He dipped his fingertips into the sandalwood and rosewater oil and massaged every part of my body. Passion, sweat, heat, intensity, lust, and love engulfed us as we devoured one another.

I came to learn that making love was an art. We made love everywhere, in every possible way, in every humanly expression and position imaginable. My appetite for him was insatiable, as was his for me. The only time he wasn't inside of me was when we were eating or bathing; but even then, our bodies found a way inside one another again. I had to have him again and again; and still, that was not enough.

How could a craving like this ever end?

षड्विंशति

When we arrived at the doors to the main palace at the Red Fort in Delhi, he introduced me to his council. There were immediate needs he had to tend to. In his world, there was always much to do.

Seeing the king in court was quite astonishing.

There were two parts to the court: the Diwan-e aam (public court) and the Diwan-e khas (courtier's hall). In the courtier's court, the king sat behind a golden railing on his regal peacock throne made of precious gems set upon a raised platform and listened to everything that affected the kingdom. It was fascinating to hear of all the stories that lived within and beyond the court. The courtier's court was to litigate issues and solve problems that affected the kingdom. Women, religious masters, and courtiers shared their viewpoints and stances before the king. I entered into his private world of urgent and forbidden matters—where his other wives were kept in the dark.

I never asked, but eagerly waited to see where I would sleep. Many wives loved living in their solitary towers, for they held a power of their own within. I supposed that was their sense of freedom. But I didn't desire that. I wanted to be next to him at all times. I couldn't imagine sleeping apart from him.

When darkness set, he led me to his bedroom. A knock at the bedroom door presented a precious worn book on a silver tray. We changed out of the costumes we wore for the day and into luxurious silk pajamas and met in bed.

"Let me tell you a story, my queen. It's another fairy tale, for you live in one now and I must continue to delight you, even though your waking life is a dream. May I ask which one is the dream?" He laughed and continued. "There is a magical tale in the Mahabharata about a woman named Draupadi. Draupadi was to married to five brothers named Yudhisthira, Bhima, Arjuna, Nakula, and Sahadeva. She was a noble woman, who possessed royalty and power like no other. She devoted her entire existence to Lord Krishna. Her life had many tales because she lived so adventurously through the divine. But a time came when she was tested and challenged. And that changed her forever. And when it was over, she would never be the same."

"One day, when Draupadi was out on a walk, she was captured and taken away to a horrible king's castle. They threw her into the courtyard, where she was surrounded by a crowd of ruthless civilians. She was poked and prodded and belittled by the king and his subjects. As a last form of brutality and cruelty, they decided to undress her in front of the crowd. Draupadi held tight to her sari as she fought off the men. But she was unable to fight against their strength and force. She succumbed to her fear and began to believe she couldn't change their minds or her destiny. She screamed in agony to Lord Krishna to save her. But he never answered her pleas. As time dragged on, so did the brutality; her sari continued to unravel. She accepted that, in mere moments, her bare body would be seen."

I listened intently as he continued.

"Out of nowhere, Lord Krishna appeared. He began to turn her sari into a never-ending garment. No matter how many times the men tried to unravel it, it would not end."

When Krishna appeared before her, she showered him in pure anger—furious for all her begging and pleading. How was it that Krishna couldn't hear her and answer her? She questioned his bravery as a god, for he did nothing to save her. Lord Krishna explained that when she called out to him, she couldn't hear him. She was gripping her sari so tight that her ego was unwilling to release itself to universal consciousness; therefore, she could not trust. Until she lost all sense of herself and her ego, he couldn't come to her, to be one with her—to show her soul the way. He replied, 'How could I have saved you? There was no space for me to enter. If you have no space within your own heart for love of the self, then how can you surrender to something or someone you have never known or trusted?'"

How can you love another unconditionally if you have never even loved yourself? The king told me tales that let me play in worlds that were far beyond me. He said he did so to make my world colorful and rich—complex with diversity and a wide spectrum of thought. He exposed every part of himself—his most vulnerable thoughts and rawest unfiltered emotions.

This allowed me to do the same.

That night, we made love numerous times.

I stayed awake after, watching as he slept. My Bengal owl, "Whoo," flew in and whispered in my ear that soon I was to be gifted. I couldn't distinguish my dreams from reality—a battle that ravished me.

सप्तविंशति

The gift was my first child. It was mesmerizing to watch my body change, transforming in ways that I never thought possible. My hair grew to great lengths and my breasts filled with fertility. I loved carrying a child. I was amazed when I could feel another heartbeat—life within life. It bewildered me how a child could live in the womb without air and survive on its mother's prana (vital life force).

I grew extremely fond of the king's first wife, Kandahari. The tower in which she lived was artistically astonishing. She had a fascinating eye that encountered many universes and she transcended them into her art and aesthetics. As the intimacy of our friendship unravelled, she spoke of her wonderful childhood and how she was born a princess of the prominent Safavid Dynasty—until the empire fell and her father fled with some of their dignitaries to India. She said that when one faces life and death as a child, existence is seen through a new set of eyes. Innocent eyes are robbed by brutality and must find innocence again in order to heal. When they arrived in India, her father befriended Akbar the Great, who introduced Shah Jahan and Kandahari into a marriage of alliance.

She stared at my stomach sadly.

I didn't know if it was because she was without child or if I had picked up on something else. "May I ask you something?"

"Anything that your heart desires. Arjumand, I am without secrets with you. For you allow me to be who I am in my truth, therefore there is nothing to hide." That was what was so beautiful about Kandahari: she spoke without thought; her words came from her heart. I never felt that kind of freedom with the king's other wife, Akbarabadi. There was always a distance between us; therefore, I kept my space.

"Why did you never bear a child?"

"I am not without a child. I don't know why this took place or how it's allowed, but it is customary. I had no choice or voice in such matters. As soon as I gave birth to Parhez Banu Begum, my daughter was immediately entrusted to Akbar's first chief wife, Ruqaiya Sultan Begum. She was told by an astrologer that she need not worry about being childless. She raised the king until he was thirteen years of age, and then he was given to his biological mother, Taj."

I looked at her with sad eyes. I couldn't imagine such a fate. I put her hand on my stomach. "Well, now we have one in the palace that we can share."

Maybe that's why she collected so many cats. She was trying to acquire as many souls as she could for the one she could never have.

On March 30th, 1613, I gave birth to Hur-al-nisa Begum, "splendid companion of paradise." The delivery was without complications, but it took a great deal of time to heal and replenish the blood I lost.

The king adored our daughter, but not like me.

There is no connection like that of a mother and a child. When a child comes to you as cosmic energy and lives in your womb for nine months, and you release them into the world, the bond is eternal. Even though the cord is cut, it is always invisibly there.

I saw life through my daughter's eyes—innocent and new. It was heavenly to breastfeed her in silence on the sunny rooftops and watch as the world passed us by. It bewildered me how still I became as the world moved before me in chaos.

Kandahari would join me. We would have beautiful conversations about philosophy and the arts and everything we thought and felt about life. We spent endless hours painting and reading to one another. She loved my daughter so much and I entrusted her with my life. I learned during this time that love only allows for one to create with love. The very essence and elixir of life can only be found with one ingredient: the hypnotic effects from the drug called **love**. It sprinkles itself everywhere and is never-ending without judgement.

I came to see that love has many changing faces.

I began to feel something toward Kandahari that I never experienced before. While soaking in the bath, I saw Kandahari watching me. There were many times I watched her as she watched me. She leaned against the wall admiring me as I sponged my body, not uttering a word. Our connection was so deep that words ceased to exist. We transcended our feelings by energy and the stories our eyes told.

I stepped out of the bath and walked across the marble floor, leaving a path of wetness. I locked the door and walked up behind her, tucking the hairs that fell out of place behind her delicate ears. She didn't know what to say or what to do––neither did I. All I could feel was our energy being transformed.

She let out a sigh.

I didn't know if it was from pleasure or relief. Slowly, I started to disrobe her; her silk sari fell on the floor like the tale the king told me about Drupadi. Maybe that was who she was in another lifetime. It was as though she was half-human and half-goddess, a demi-god.

Something about her was untouchable.

There was a rawness to her regality.

She wore no undergarments; her breasts were divine. Her skin felt heavenly to touch. I didn't know what I was doing or why I was doing it, but it felt right. I wondered what it was like when the king had her. Did she moan in ecstasy as I did? Or did she contain herself as she always did when she was in his presence?

I led her to the bath, where we sat for hours talking about life, death, and everything in between. Afterwards, we went outside for a shirodhara (*shiro* [head], *dhara* [flow]) with warm coconut oil to massage our third eye and awaken the chakras of our scalps. Sitting beneath the willow tree, mustard oil flowed onto our third eye and was massaged into our scalps. I spoke of the willow tree's wisdom and how as a child we had one at the palace that was said to be magical.

अष्टाविंशति

I received a letter stating the king requested me at battle. This was the first one I was to attend. I don't believe in war, which made it difficult to go. Thoughts of separation from my daughter weighed heavily on my heart. But I would never bring her along. I could never put her in harm's way. Nor would I want her to be in that energy, even though she would have no recollection of it.

I asked Kandahari and Teetu to keep a watchful eye on her as I traveled to the Rajput state of Menwar. Sadness grew with each step the elephant took, knowing that my daughter was farther and farther away. I looked at paintings of her that I had painted in my sketchbook and strands of her baby hair that I collected. The feeling of these tactile memories helped to heal my aching heart. My lap felt so empty. My hands felt like they were missing something.

I tried to distract them with the intricate drawings of the present battle. I was amazed to see the size of the army that the king amassed and the number of cannons that were to be used, not to mention the number of cavalry and elephants. During Akbar's reign, the protocol for battle was to encamp for some weeks facing your rival at a distance, not proceeding until a move was made by the opposition. Sneak attacks were never used; his dear friend Abdul Fazl called such behavior "a trade among cowards."

After weeks of travel, I arrived.

The king was the first to greet me. He led me to his quarters and served me a decadent lunch, which he fed to me. It didn't even feel as if we were at a battle.

"How was your journey, Mumtaz?"

"It was long and difficult to leave her. I am blessed that we have such wonderful hands to watch over her. Knowing I was to be with you made the treacherous journey worthwhile."

He delicately kissed my lips and looked into my eyes.

"The battle is days away. Did you see the drawings? What did you think of my idea? I have decided that the men will stand behind the cannons and keep watch. When the moment is right, we will proceed into battle atop cavalry. As you have advised, this will save many lives and animals."

"As you know, I do not believe in war, but I think it's a bold move. The cannons can breach the fort walls due to their strength and if the timing is calculated with precision, you will have the time it takes to reload. It will also give you an upper hand with swords and bows and arrows. Many lives will be spared, which means the most to me."

The king was a man who went into battle with practical ideologies; he was not a dreamer seeking an impossible dream. That was what made him a warrior. He never hid behind a curtain. His presence was always seen.

The following days were immersed by battle. The sounds of the deafening cannons and brutal warfare broke my heart.

You could hear the horrific screams of warriors gasping for their last breaths of life and the smell death. I even began to hear death in moments of silence. I chanted spiritual sutras relentlessly, asking for grace and forgiveness in such darkness. I could feel the pain inflicted upon Mother Earth as we beat her, and the universe's tears from all the bloodshed.

All I could do was walk back and forth, as I wasn't allowed to leave the grounds at any time. The king wouldn't have it, even though the fort was guarded.

I had a lot of time to think.

During those moments of stillness and silence, an idea came to me. I began to compile many ideas, which turned into a chronicle called the Aminai Qazvini. It spoke of love, war, vices, and the arts. It was to be highly controversial, as it was written with many voices and many visions. I penned some with anonymous names, as they stirred the king's political pot. I knew that my soul's purpose was to give a voice to the voiceless; that could never be taken from me.

Every obstacle is an opportunity for transformation.

The cover story was about a man who went into battle for his king and never returned. He was sent to fight for his king despite moral objections. He died next to his best friend, his horse, who wept for days until he, too, died from bloodshed. I questioned the meaning and price of life.

Was it all predestined?

Was it all man's choice?

Why would God allow such a fate? Did God make men actors for his amusement for some unknown deeper meaning?

Did man make his own rules and turn a blind eye to God in the pursuit of power and reign?

What about free choice? Did we not have the right to choose what we believed? Are we not all born of many faiths and faces in every birth we take? If love is the core of all religions, then how can we act with such brutality?

In another article, I spoke of domination and the desire to rule and control others through religious faith. War is all about power and man's interpretation of religion. A common rationale for religious disputes is separation and differences: the Muslim religion was defined by a day of judgement by one god, Allah; the Hindus believed in infinite limitlessness through multiple deities. Cages and limits against unlimited freedom.

But what if we became like Akbar? What if we became tolerant and embraced our differences with love?

I wrote a tale I heard about Akbar and how he became a devotee of the Hindu god, Durga, after marrying a Hindu princess. It was believed by Akbar that he was a Hindu in his previous birth named Mukunda Brahmachari and, by mistake, he consumed a cow's hair while drinking milk and committed suicide. For this, he was reincarnated as a mlechchha (non-Hindu). Since he knew the core of all religions was love, he rejoiced all faiths and visions. He created a breathtaking temple named Bhadrakali, which was situated in Rajasthan's Hanumangarh district.

By the end of the battle, the king led 200,000 men to victory and King Maharana Amar Singh II surrendered. Before we were to set foot, I made sure that all the dead were buried. Even though the king opposed the idea, he fulfilled my wishes. I didn't enforce it for disease control, but for being ethically human. No being deserves to die in the first place and no being deserves to be left in such a ruthless state.

एकान्नत्रिंशत्

The king and I explored magical places and mystical temples as we made our way back. We began by bathing in an enchanted crystal cave under a million stars that glimmered like diamonds as our elephants joyfully swam. Being in water helped to heal the aches that set into my heart from the warfare. As we made our way through the jungle, there was a beautiful deserted temple where I could feel djinns walking by. I watched as tigers sat under ancient trees that spoke their scrolls through their trunks, while monkeys playfully chased each other. When I closed my eyes and meditated, the energy was so profound that I felt infinitesimal. Nature and animals have always been my healing talisman. I never knew how the king found such enchanting places. What he showed me, and what I experienced, baffled those with rare eyes who had seen it all.

He knew the unknown.

When we arrived home, I immediately ran up the palace stairs so I could hold my daughter. Tears of happiness streamed down my cheeks with a mixture of sadness because I knew that so many children and animals lost their families.

I could feel Kandahari by the door.

I didn't even need to see her to feel her presence.

"I missed you dearly, Kandahari. How did you keep your days while I was away?"

"I entertained myself in the gardens and kept a watchful eye on Hur-al-nissa. Are you okay? I see that sadness has set into your eyes. I don't know what to say, as I have never experienced what you have. So, I am without words."

Although we were both married to the king, our lives were different in every conceivable way.

"I question why I went, especially because I do not believe in war. Was I being a dutiful wife? To silently heal? To hope my thoughts and presence could stop a battle? I once heard a story of a mystic who believed that he controlled battles with his thoughts in meditation. Maybe I thought I could do the same. I don't know how to answer such questions. But an idea came to me: to create a chronicle for those who have been silenced. I may not be able to reform all that is around me, but I can define the inner strength that lives within all of us, universally, with a voice. Then compassion may have a chance. Perhaps you want to share a story. I'm asking everyone for their experiences so we can grow and learn from one another. War is complicated. As is the human mind. I will leave it at that."

My stomach felt queasy and nauseous. I assumed that maybe it was the lingering expression of the war within me. But as the king and I made love during the war, a seed of life was created.

I gave birth to Jahanara Begum, on March 23th, 1614. She was a beautiful child. She had black locks that shone blue in the light and eyes like the cosmos. I knew that she was an old soul. She held a wisdom that was beyond this life.

The king adored her.

They had an unexplainable connection. He always wanted to be close to her and hold her. It was surprising, as he didn't have a similar bond with our other daughter or any of the other children he fathered. After we married, he never slept in another bed and none of his other wives got pregnant.

Four months after I birthed Jahanara, I was told that I was pregnant. I was surprised, as I waited months before the king and I made love so my body could heal. I practiced a lot of yoga and meditated and allowed my body to rest as much as it could, as it had not recovered from the last birth. On March 20th, 1615, I gave birth to my first son—Dara Shukoh, "as magnificent as Darius."

For weeks, I was advised to stay in bed. I bled more and more with each birth. The doctors noted that I hemorrhaged. Thoughts of distress and pain never occupied my mind, even if my body felt it, because I wouldn't succumb to it; after all, I was swarmed in love. Even bedridden, we played an array of imaginary games. Every night, I would tell them a mystical tale of the universe as we laid in bed; and when they woke, they would curl into my body as we silently watched the sunrise. The children brought such joy to my world that my body quickly healed. I instilled in them since their first breath that life holds more than what the eyes can see. There is magic beyond the known senses; for the universe holds its truth in the invisible, but not all are granted the permission to see it.

त्रिंशत्

It was a beautiful morning. I excitedly went to Jahanara and Dara's bedrooms to kiss them good morning. I walked over to Hur-al-Nissa's bed to find her covered in vomit. I picked her up; she had a severe fever. I immediately called for Wazir Khan. When he arrived, he told me that her face and body would be covered in blisters and sores in the following weeks. She had contracted smallpox. I collapsed to the floor and tears flooded my eyes like a monsoon as I shrieked in pain.

The palace shook.

The king ran in, but I couldn't speak.

I locked the door and would not allow anyone to enter.

I bathed her body in sandalwood to relieve the excruciating pain and read her stories as I cradled her to soothe the sorrow. I tried to hold my tears back; and when the moments were too overbearing, she saw what I wished she had not. After a week, the pustules and blisters moved from her face to her body. Her scabs and boils were so sharp I could feel them pierce through my skin as I cradled her in my arms.

She became unrecognizable.

My heart broke into pieces. I couldn't understand how an innocent child could be destined with such a horrific fate.

How could I, as a mother, be so helpless?

I knew that Jahanara and Dara missed me dearly because they would speak to me through the door. I tried to be with them as much as I could through the door's barrier—explaining the unexplainable as best as I could. Children have a better understanding of death and the invisible because they haven't become attached to the illusions of life.

Not even for a moment did I leave her side.

Love never disappears.

Her little body was dying as it tried to hold on. She barely slept. I didn't sleep either, for I felt her pain. I knew that she was enduring tremendous pain so that she could be with me. I couldn't let go; therefore, she couldn't move on.

But I had to.

God spoke to me through her.

It was the early hours of the morning. I could tell because we hadn't slept for sixteen days. She laid atop my chest, staring deep into my eyes as I sang to her. As she gently closed her eyes, her breath got lighter and lighter. I wanted to breathe life into her, but I knew I could not. It was time to release her; she needed to be freed. I knew it was her last breath, for she opened her eyes and spread her tiny hands over my heart.

When she died, my heart stopped.

A part of my soul died.

Sadness and anger competed for space in my heart.

I only experienced death through my animals, my beloved
Looki and Moksha; but I was far too young to understand the
depth and meaning of death. My heart didn't know that a pain
like this could exist—until now. I wouldn't allow anyone to
enter as I held her lifeless body for days. I cradled her in my
arms, begging the gods to answer me; they did not.

The king was at the door, sitting in a chair, waiting for me.
I didn't know how he knew when I was leaving, as I never
spoke a word. His unconditional love let him feel my immense
sorrow. He could walk inside my body and feel what I felt. He
allowed me to grieve naturally, the way I needed to. He didn't
speak to ease my moments of sadness and stillness. He allowed
me to find my way while silently guiding me.

"Mumtaz, sometimes the gods have plans that are
unknown to us. Sometimes, there is reasoning and forces far
beyond what is known—where words can't explain the
unexplainable."

In order to heal my energy, I immersed myself in creative
writing. Creativity was my outlet for pain; it was my rebellion
against death. I wrote every idea and thought that crossed my
mind. The chronicles became published across India. Ideas, no
matter their public perception, were shared. The pursuit of
justice and a humane way of life became the foundation of my
voice. There was no discrepancy with caste or social status.
Widows, the underprivileged, and animals were cared for and
sheltered. The king's associates were shocked by my manners.
To allow a woman to have such a strong voice and make such
powerful choices was unheard of.

During this time, the king appointed me his imperial seal, the Muhr Uzah—a title bestowed to no other woman. The king supported everything I did, even if he didn't understand my reasoning; I reciprocated his unconditional support. We solidified our bond and connection to a higher realm through compassion and conscious love for one another.

I waited quite some time before I was ready to bury our daughter in the gardens of paradise. I needed time and space. And when I did, I buried a piece of my soul, knowing what I had lost could never be reclaimed, though I would continue to search for it for lifetimes.

I sat for days in solitude in the gardens of paradise and watched as leaves fell to the earth. Roses blossomed and petals fell. Slowly, I began to discover the beauty of living when I faced death without fear or sadness; that is when I saw that life lived within death. The healing energy of Mother Nature is unfathomable, as is a child's innocent laughter.

एकत्रिंशत्

I was six weeks pregnant when the king and I were to travel. Journeying great distances through a variety of climates proved difficult, especially atop an elephant. Exploring the world with the children filled me with a sense of wonder. Our eyes and minds were opened to new dimensions of life; every region of India is rich and diverse in food, culture, and topography. I saw visions and life through their eyes. There was an innocence in which they lived that I was still learning to rebirth. As much as I had healed, a faint scar of death lingered; and because of that fear crept in if I didn't control and discipline my thoughts. I didn't want to pass this vibration on to my newborn, for all that I felt, saw, thought, and created would be passed onto my invisible child when it was time to take birth, for energy never dies.

On June 23th, 1616, I gave birth to my fourth child, Shah Shuja. Thankfully, it was an uncomplicated pregnancy. After bearing four children, I still couldn't fathom how a child begins as a seed in the womb, then begins to nourish on milk, and shortly thereafter begins to crawl. The process of life baffled me. In the blink of an eye, they were running from room to room. Their first sounds spoke of their inner worlds. It made me wonder how thoughts are formed, where they came from, and how the universe creates such uniqueness.

As they slowly started to become their own beings, I could see a beautiful reflection of us in each of them. Though I could see more of the king's face in Jahanara, she had more of my heart. Even as a baby she always wanted to be of service. I always wondered if children chose us or if we chose them—or if all of it was predestined and an executed plan by God.

I was still breastfeeding Shah Shuja when Wazir Khan performed a check-up and told me that I was pregnant. I couldn't believe it. The king and I only made love once and I even began to take mild doses of neem as a contraceptive. I asked Wazir Khan repeatedly to check his diagnosis, but each time he had the same answer.

The beginning months went with bliss, but as the days went on, deep complications arose. I began to spot and then I lost vast amounts of blood. Wazir Khan said it was nothing dire: normal complications that were the offset of multiple back-to-back pregnancies.

But I was ordered to be bedrest.

Jahanara never left my side. Tears flooded my face when I heard that she began to offer jewels to the poor in hopes her offerings would appease the gods and restore my health. She was such a unique child; her love didn't see with the eyes, it saw with the soul.

I began to have vivid dreams, which led to a dream that the child I was carrying was a poet named Mirabai who died in ancient Dwarka in 1557. Dwarka was an enchanted place like no other. There are turquoise sunken cities with elaborate shrines below the sea and masterpiece stone structures and temples underground.

Mirabai's life began so magically. She was born an aristocratic, mystical songstress devoted to Lord Krishna. When Mirabai was a child, a Sadhu walked through her village and stumbled upon her father and her. The Sadhu was a very wise man who was connected to the gods. He looked into Mirabai's eyes and saw Lord Krishna and knew that immediately he had to bestow the Krishna doll he had in his hands upon her, saying the doll was destined to be in her hands. Her father took the doll home, thinking it would be best to wait some time before giving the godly gift to his daughter. But Mirabai immediately asked her father for it; and with that, it was hers. Mirabai fell deeply in love with Lord Krishna. She dedicated every breath and poetic bhajan (devotional songs of God) to him. Her world was painted in ecstasy for Lord Krishna.

As she grew older, she was questioned by her mother about who she was to marry. She replied, "Why would I need a husband? I have my beloved, Lord Krishna."

When the time arrived, a prince named Bhoj Raj was found and she was to be married. Mirabai was not taken by her elevated social position or the many luxuries that surrounded her. Her husband's family grew enraged as she continued to worship Lord Krishna while they worshipped Durga. However, that didn't stop Mirbai's profound expression of love for her master.

Her husband's jealously grew.

When he heard she was entertaining other men in her quarters, he stormed in and found her reciting mantras of bliss to her doll. Knowing he could never own her heart, he set her free to live in her divineness.

Mirabai wandered and continued to unravel the mysteries of the universe; it was said that the cosmos spoke through her eyes. Word traveled all over India about Mirabai being a saint. It was even spoken that Akbar came to see her, disguised as a Sadhu, as the families were rivals. He heard that her musical expressions were that of a god, and for that he placed priceless jewels upon her feet.

Prince Bhoj Raj heard word of his wife's omnipotence and called for her. When he set eyes upon her, he profusely apologized for his ignorance. She went back to the palace to live with the king and his family.

Shortly after, he died in battle.

Her father-in-law, Rana Sanga, demanded that she commit Sati (when one commits suicide by throwing their body upon a pyre). Mirabai rejected Sati, as she stated that her beloved, Lord Krishna, had not died. Her in-laws became crueler to her; many more attempts were made on her life, even poisonous concoctions. Mirabai was told by a trusted seer that she must escape.

It was said that she died the way a saint does. Before her last breath, Lord Krishna came before her and opened his heart and she melted into Krishna consciousness.

On September 3rd, 1617, I gave birth to Roshanara Begum. She was a mystical child. As soon as she took her first breath, poetic beauty flowed into the world.

द्वात्रिंशत्

The king and I wanted to make love as soon as my body healed. Even when I was in pain, I craved him. It was a craving that never stopped. There is something about being deeply intertwined with another soul. Words cease to exist, and only the body and silence can express what is felt. When you fall so deeply in love with another, you lose yourself within them, for you are each other's mirror, reflecting love off one another. It would seem to an outsider as a love from the divine, god to goddess.

The expressions of our love changed like the scenery we experienced. We were never the same person or energy twice.

On November 3rd, 1618, I gave birth to Aurangzeb. Since his first breath, he was a daring child. He did as he pleased. I knew as he grew, he would be his own ruler and others would have no say in what he did or what he would become. There is a look in a child's eyes, even when they are innocent, that a mother can feel. For the eyes speak truthfully before they become worldly.

I didn't understand why I felt such sharps pains in my stomach and retained an exorbitant amount of fluid. When I questioned Wazir Khan, he proceeded with an intense check-up, announcing that I was pregnant once more. I didn't know how my body was going to make it. I couldn't imagine going through another pregnancy. Every time I gave birth, it seemed as though I was being depleted of every morsel of energy, vitamin, strength, and force that existed in my body.

I knew the king had to travel for some campaigns. If I spoke of my pain, he would stay back to tend to me and I didn't want him to do so. So, I bit my cheeks in anguish and tried to sleep as much as I could as we trekked atop elephant. Many times, I had to ask that we stop due to sickness, as it became unbearable. The king suggested that we turn back, but I wouldn't allow him to do so. He always tended to me in such a tender way—offering me this, doing that, speaking words of sweetness, anything he could conjure to elevate my suffering.

As soon as we reached the palace, the help lifted me off the elephant to a canopy bed that looked out the window onto the garden and grounds. The children kept themselves amused playing in the mystical playground. I would talk to them through the window, pretending I was there with them. I wanted to be as attentive and present as I could. Jahanara was always dutiful by my side, keeping a watchful eye upon the other children. She took my place in many ways, from assuming my role as first lady to serving her father in the courts and even in the construction of military campaigns.

I barely slept and anxiousness was the only feeling I knew as I awaited my delivery date. Teetu was always conjuring new recipes, trying to find a specialty that would ease my distress or at the very least put a faint smile of gratitude on my face. Though I couldn't eat, I deeply appreciated his attempts. My feet and legs were so swollen that they looked as if I had a fatal disease. The help constantly massaged them and lathered them with special ointments, which didn't help.

The only one who knew the true depth of my pain was Wazir Khan. I secretly asked for mild sedations, as death had crept into my body as I laid in corpse pose. I made sure all of his remedies and what he administered was natural, as I always wanted my body pure. The only thing that momentarily alleviated the pain was when I called to out to the gods.

On December 18th, 1619, I could barely breathe as copious amounts of blood seeped out of my body. I pushed and pushed and nothing but fluids of horrific colors came out of me. I pushed so hard that there was nothing that I could push, even when I had been told to stop hours before.

"Mumtaz, please stop pushing. There is nothing to push."

Wazir quietly spoke that I had lost this child. I will never understand how death found me again, even though a part of me knew.

He never breathed.

He never drank from my breasts.

He never spoke his name.

He never got to crawl.

He never celebrated a birthday.

He never heard me say "I love you," though my tears spoke the words.

I was told Izad Bakhsh died of unknown causes.

How does a child die of unknown causes? How can the universe allow for brutality to such innocence? I began to see that giving birth to a child and releasing it into an uncontrollable world is a form of death.

I cried uncontrollably.

I cried for what I couldn't have.

I cried for what I lost.

My heart bled so much it stopped beating. The gods felt it. When you love so deeply, you suffer profusely from its depth. I knew I could connect to my children in the ethereal—through spirit—but that held no solace. I yearned to hold them in my arms and to feel their energy, to touch their skin, to hear their breath, and to look into their eyes.

The king saw sadness had settled in my eyes. The eyes speak of life and the experiences it holds and cannot let go of. He suggested that I begin a spiritual quest to understand Tantric magic and yoga. This was so that I could become one with death's magic—to learn how to live in death, so I could live. Otherwise, I would be in agony, peeling my heart off of the marble floor for all of eternity, as I had been doing.

Perhaps he wanted me to attain Moksha (liberation). However, that didn't exist in the Tantra. Tantra states that all is perfectly divine as it is, even the self. It was hard for me to believe that everything was perfect, especially myself, after the devastating deaths of my beloved children. I was not free; death chained me and my emotions consumed me. When you miscarry or lose a child, you begin to blame yourself in one form or another. As a mother you feel helpless, even when you know that there is nothing you could have done to change God's course.

The king gifted me with a Siddha, "perfected one." Siddhas broke mans illusionary attachments through yoga and mystical states to become perfected masters. A true Siddha, on Earth, is a pure incarnation of the gods.

I was amazed when I saw a corpse-like, frail man with matted hair in front of me. He wore giant bone hoops in his ears that went through his cartilage; it was said that his ears were cut open with a dagger during initiation. He sat in the gardens doing hatha yoga around a fire he built with a skull begging bowl. He practiced Hatha yoga because it induces the state of spiritual perfection: the mind leaves the physical plane and becomes "union through discipline."

We didn't exchange a word.

We had nothing to say and he remained silent for decades.

Meditation and Shiva's 112 techniques were prescribed as my cure for death's disease. We used Vedic breathing techniques, such as Pranayama, to dispel fear and expand the self. I began to connect with the energy of kundalini (serpent power) and dug deeply into my Manipura (Mani [gem], Pura [city]), my second mind—the lotus within my navel. It was told that I could find the answers there.

There were many forms and ways in which I expressed what lived within my soul. In the beginning, all I could do was cry and yell from the pain. The pain was so deep I wondered when it would stop. I wondered how many lifetimes it had accumulated from, for it seemed as if it came from an endless tunnel. I allowed myself to be vulnerable to my truth and whatever lived in me to come out so I could be natural and

free—so I didn't have to suppress myself. Otherwise, I would
be hiding from myself from here to eternity, and that would
create a sickness or disease of the mind-body that would
become uncurable over time. I came to understand through
the unspoken words of the Siddha that the mind and body are
one; and when they become separate, that is when disorder
and disease begins. I was taught that the silence of the mind
transcends emotions into nothingness—no mind, no body. I
never knew there were so many ancient techniques prescribed
to find the silent watcher who watches within.

त्रयत्रिंशत्

The limestone Rohtasgarh Fort was enchanting, as were the Persians gardens and the Ganesh temple. It was located on the serene banks of the Sone River Valley and surrounded by two hundred waterfalls and dense forestry. Wildlife existed everywhere. The healing energy of nature has always been my calling, which was why I was to give birth here.

The king revolted against his father, another reason why we took refuge here. The king and his father had a complicated relationship that turned volatile as time went on. Jahangir requested that the king step into another combat, but the king was situated in a current campaign here. The king arranged for everything to be taken care of for his father's battle, which turned out to be disastrous. Nur Jahan's constant thirst for political prestige didn't help, either. Especially since Jahangir gave her unchecked power.

Death and blood would flow.

The world outside was rapidly changing; religious tolerance wasn't as prevalent as it once was. I wanted the children to know tolerance and acceptance of other beliefs in the world, as they were young and impressionable. I knew the children's minds were like a canvas: whatever I painted upon it since birth would be the mirror that would be reflected. Even at such a young age, we allowed the children to discover what they desired. Nothing was forced upon them or made mandatory.

They had only rule: to follow the truth of their hearts. I never stopped them from their truth, even as babies. If they wanted to express tears or a story, I allowed them to do so. I believe that as soon as a child is imprinted with a lie, or led astray from their truth of expression, they become lost and the personal identity has now been stamped with a trademark that may lead them to a life that was not destined for their purpose. Listening with love was the greatest gift I could give them. My parents raised me this way, and I saw the beauty of unconditional love. We raised our children in a kingdom of freedom and love.

I was in the gardens painting the trees and elephants with the children when an excruciating pain on my right side began. I grasped my stomach and began to chant to the gods relentlessly. It was a feeling I experienced too many times before and was horrified to be introduced to again.

I clenched onto the sheets and gritted my teeth in pain as I chanted to the gods and delivered my daughter, Surya. Submerged in such darkness, I had to find the light as the Tantra stated. So, I named her after the Hindu god of divine light, the glorious sun. For weeks on end, I was advised to drink bitter turmeric tea to flush out my internals as my body laid inflamed in corpse pose. Breastfeeding was arduous and painful. My nipples were so raw they bled.

I continued to practice active meditation in bed and dedicate myself to deepening my yogic breath in order to heal my body. I knew the deeper my breath, the more oxygen and life-force there would be toward healing. When Wazir Khan said that my health was restored, I was excited to experience life once again. But that was taken away very quickly. All that I would see for the rest of the year would be that which existed in my bedroom from a window. When you are confined and look outside a window, even if it's the most beautiful window, you feel like a prisoner.

Even as a seed within my womb, I felt as if my child was without a heartbeat—though I was told otherwise. I tried to convince myself with the thoughts of others that maybe my past experiences and tragedies had crept into my mind again. Month after month, I watched obsessively as my belly barely grew.

When it came time to give birth, I had already surrendered to death. I knew that my child was taken long before and had gone to the gods. My head lady-in-waiting, Sati-un-Nisa Khanam, tried to comfort me as best she could when she cut the umbilical cord, but the cord was cut long ago. Wazir Khan pulled my child's bloody, lifeless body from my womb. I didn't even cry; there were no more tears within for what I had suffered. I cradled his body in my arms for days and chanted rituals of love. Maybe I made it harder on myself in doing so, but there was no other way for me to let go.

I did what I had to.

I had to live in my truth.

When he was laid to rest in his marble tomb, endless tears dropped upon his face like they had for all of the other children. I released my child into the ethereal—laying him to rest in the gardens of paradise. I begged the gods to answer my pleas as to why I endured such unthinkable suffering and pain.

Silently, I questioned God's choices and decisions.

What had I done unknowingly in my previous birth? What karma did my children have to pay, from past births, for having such a fate? What lessons was I to learn?

Every night I cuddled up to the king, searching for the answers to life and death. He spoke of how Krishna explains that rebirth is when a being picks up from their previous death. The next birth they are born into has the same state of mind they had before death, as well as their karma and Runa (debt). The time given and the reason why some never take a breath is because of their karmic cycle and the debt to the family that had to be repaid to break the karmic cycle. His faith was much stronger than mine in this regard. He lived knowing that life and death were one. He said death balanced life, and that was the duality of life.

"Mumtaz, how does one know a blessing or the true meaning of life unless the opposite is experienced to the fullest depths? Life has many experiences. You come to understand the meaning of life through the journey. Self-realization is found there; and within that, you will find your soul's purpose."

I secretly wondered why pain was needed in any form.

चतुस्त्रिंशत्

We were to travel to Mandu Shadiabad (city of joy) located in ancient Madhya Pradesh, where the king had another campaign. The Jahaz Mahal, "ship palace," was a marvelous palace because of the illusion of its reflection, which looked like a ship floating on a lake. The pools on the rooftop were heavenly. The king and I swam as gods and goddesses beneath the stars.

The Jahaz Mahal was built during the reign of Mandu Sultan Ghiyas-ud-din Khilji, a pleasure-seeking king who adored women and music. His harem boasted 15,000 women, for which he had to build a second palace.

How does one man have such time to entertain so many women? Was he so bored with the female species that none could quench his thirst for lust and love? I never understood why he accumulated such a collection. Some of the women he acquired even went into battle.

When I questioned the king, he said that love is rare to find. Many seek impossible questions and answers of the self in others, without knowing who they are, and they will never find it in another, so they keep looking for lifetimes.

"To find all that you seek within one being is impossible, and in doing so it will lead you to insanity. Two souls have to know their true inner being and become one. And to walk such a cosmic journey is unheard of, except for the few that are cherished even after centuries. That is how rare and powerful love is."

On October 8th, 1624, I gave birth with ease to Murad Baksh, which meant wanted, desired, and omnipotent. They say that when you bestowed this sacred name upon a child, you ensured that they will outlive their parent's legacy—which became my greatest wish. My body healed almost seamlessly, which allowed for me to embark on a sacred journey.

Spiritually, I had been preparing for a long-awaited pilgrimage. Twelve years for the auspicious time when the sun, moon, and Jupiter were perfectly intertwined. I was to trek with Ganesh to the four sacred rivers—Haridwar on the Ganges, Ujjain on the Shipra, Nashik on Godavari, and Prayag for Kumbh Mela. The myth of the Kumbh Mela was that gods and demons went to battle over amrita, the elixir of immorality. In doing so, the four sacred rivers became nectar, which allowed mortals to bathe in God's purity.

Endless faces and bodies of Sadhus (holy men), ascetics, and enlightened beings came together for seventy-five days to wash their souls of unholy ways in the holy waters and become reborn once again. When my body went beneath the holy waters of the Ganges, I felt as if I had doused myself in the sacred nectar of the gods.

I would offer myself to the gods daily.

The air I breathed was otherworldly, omnipotent.

Many days were spent in silence. In silence, I could turn off the channels of thoughts that proved to lead nowhere and hear myself, and listen to my inner voice. This allowed me to release the remaining pain and karma that unconsciously lived within me. There is something very powerful and vulnerable in letting go and surrendering your spirit to the universe— releasing past lives, present pains, and the unknown.

I wrote the king many letters because I missed him and the children dearly. Being alone, although chaperoned, was very healing for me. No other queen was allowed such freedom. I could step away from what I was, what I heard, and what I lived in to become a blank canvas among the masses that sought the divine.

I saw who I was when I was alone.

In my aloneness, I learned the difference between loneliness and being alone, and how to fall in love with my own company without having to entertain myself with outside distractions. I did copious amounts of yoga—so much, that I felt as though I had become the air I breathed. I came to understand through meditation that I could die and take birth, all within the same body. I wasn't who I once was. I wasn't what I lived. I could become whomever I desired. I became nothingness in the universe's silence.

I slept so deeply that I entered into the state of yoga nidra, where the body ceases to dream or live out the unlived desires of the subconscious through dreams. Every moment of those seventy-five days was spent in religious and spiritual attainment, even whilst sitting in lotus pose laughing and drinking chai.

When I returned to the palace, it was different. It's not that the palace had changed, it was that I had changed within. I had shed many layers of skin. I don't know how to explain it, but it felt as though the Ganges washed away my pain—that my darkness had flowed down the river.

The king admired my newfound strength and wisdom. Many times, there was nothing for me to say, as my eyes were so deep and full that they spoke for me. Even the children knew what I thought or the answers to their questions by the way my eyes fell upon them. We painted and created, watched great theatrical pieces; I had great insights and inspirations that served humanity. The simplicity of life awed me. Life was magical. I lived within my moments. I was present to the present. I sought joy without expectations of the past or the future.

When Wazir said I was pregnant again, I felt blissful and connected. On November 4th, 1626, I gave birth to Luft Allah, which meant joy and happiness.

पञ्चत्रिंशत्

We were to journey to Shahi Qila, a majestic fort in Burhanpur. The fort's exterior was constructed of blue Persian Kashi tiles that were so spellbinding that it took your breath away. The entrance of the fort faced the lavish blue, green, and yellow Maryam Zamani Mosque, with Quranic and non-Quranic inscriptions. You could see Hindu architecture all around, especially in the zoomorphic corbels. The Almagiri gates opened to Hazuri Bagh, spectacular gardens that the children and I adored. From there, you could always see the stunning Badshahi mosque. It was situated on the north bank of the Tapti River and originally built by Farooqui rulers.

It took Akbar 11 months to conquer Burhanpur. It became a place where princes and ambassadors were appointed. We were to reside here for quite some time, as the king had become governor of Burhanpur. He became so fond of Shahi Qila that he established his court, the Diwan-I-Aam and Diwan-I-Khas, on the terrace of the Qila.

The Shah built a glorious Zenana Hammam for me so I could indulge in my luxurious rituals. Invigorating fragrances of saffron, khus, and rose scented the heavenly waters.

I always wondered if it was known as the "Bhulbhulaya"

(labyrinth) because it held more meaning than I knew of, for the labyrinth is the journey to one's center. A labyrinth has only one path to the center and one path out, a unicursal (one line). It was said to be the journey of life to the spiritual awakening of death.

Maybe I thought this way because shortly after I gave birth to Luft Allah, I lost him. I just didn't know that the universe was going to take two more children from me. I didn't know how to express my experiences with death and what my heart encountered. In many ways, I learned to heal death or at least silence it; in other ways, my heart was not allowed to go to the depths of its despair, in fear I may never ever come back, for that is how deeply I felt.

I took to rising at four in the morning like when I was a child. This hour of silence and magic became my time to observe the darkness breaking the light, to see a breathtaking sunrise unfold. I walked barefoot through the labyrinth, spreading my toes deep into the soil. I watched as every cell from my foot left its pattern in the dirt. I could hear the earth's echo of *Om* in the silence. I walked the labyrinth   seeking the meaning of life. The universe and I conversed. Many answers and questions were left floating within the walls.

I chanted sutras while my hands channeled mudras. Beads of sweat dripped down my body even though the sun barely rose above the horizon. My silk kurta pajamas stuck to my body like a second skin, especially against my pregnant stomach, which carried my fourteenth child.

I went into a trance and when I opened my eyes, I saw Kabir's frail shadow, like a spirit, walking toward the front entrance through the mist of the early morning. Despite his white hair and walking cane, he appeared youthful; his spirit shone brighter as his body diminished with time. I didn't know how old he was or if he was even real. Kabir smiled to himself and sang with an Indian jungle crow he picked up along the way, which now sat on his shoulder. I attempted to bow to his feet, but he wouldn't allow me to do so. He pressed his hands into prayer and graced his fingertips on my cheek, placing his third finger, scented with agar oil, in between my eyes—on my third eye. He opened his weathered palm to reveal mint leaves from his garden. He knew that pregnancy made my digestive problems even more irksome and irritable. Mint and leafy concoctions eased my nausea and helped to reduce the thickness of my blood. Sometimes, I liked to slowly chew the tart leaves; other times, I preferred them as a brewed tea. Being a seer, he blamed my ailments on the constellations of Virgo and what I failed to release from my previous births.

"Teetu, where are you?"

"Teetu, Teetu." I could hear the echoes of the younger children mimicking me as they called for Teetu.

Beautiful laughter filled the silence.

"Yes," Teetu responded. "Where are you?"

"By the front entrance."

A few moments later, he appeared and I could see the children peering around the staircase. I placed my beautiful cat, Sher (tiger), on the marble floor and playfully told her to attack the children. I watched as they ran for cover and scattered around, giggling uncontrollably as they did so. Jahanara, now seventeen, was far too refined to partake in such games—though she did play along for the children's sake. I needed laughter and Ananda (bliss) in every moment, especially after experiencing so much suffering. Being a child was my medicine; laughter was the healing cure and talisman to death.

"May we have some tea? Kabir, have you eaten?"

"I have just eaten, Arjumand, but thank you. Teetu, how are you?" Kabir asked.

"Very, very well for as long as I am here." He pointed to the sky, questioning his luck and timing. He turned dramatically and went off to make his delicacies.

We strolled through the gardens in silence. I didn't know why Kabir was here. Part of me didn't want to know. I dipped my toes in the fountains. I needed to cool off; maybe I wanted to ease my tense mind.

"Shall we sit in the shade under the peepal tree?" Peepala and Ashvattha were demons with magical powers. They would seduce innocent people into touching the peepal tree so that they could kill them. It was said that Lord Vishnu hid under this sacred tree when the demons defeated the gods. Peepala and Ashvattha were both killed by Lord Shani on an auspicious Saturday.

Coincidence or not, today was Saturday.

"How are you, Arjumand?" Kabir always called me by my given name—never Mumtaz. It was endearing and comforting to my child ears.

"I am well. And you?"

"Blessed by the gods for every last breath that is to come."

"Are you still wearing the star necklace?"

I moved my hair away from my chest and lifted it from beneath the camel-colored silk.

"Do you remember what I told you as a child? That only one thing, and one thing only, should ever change your destiny. Yet when it does, it will never, ever, be the same again. However, I never spoke the words."

"Yes," I responded, bowing my head and closing my eyes. "You wouldn't tell me why or how, but said you would appear when the time was right." I started to pour the tea, but I dropped the glass and it shattered into miniscule pieces. I knew in that moment a simple truth: Life would never be the same, for a voice inside, an omen, silently spoke.

"Are you okay?" Kabir asked.

"Oh, yes, I'm fine," I reassured him. "I'm sorry. I was taken away."

I tried to regain my composure and clean up the mess, mostly to occupy my mind. I pulled some leaves off the godly tree and placed them on my hand.

His voice softened. "The time will come soon, Arjumand."

"What do you mean? What time will come soon?"

"I must tell you now, for I have waited far too long. I did not know how to speak such words. I tried everything that I could, every plea, begging, and offering that I knew. I set out to find you many times and turned away. I still don't know how to speak such words. I hoped that somewhere along the way my prayers would have been heard and the gods would prove me wrong—that this foretelling was just a disguise all along."

I looked down at the dirt, avoiding eye contact. Did I know then that this was my final resting place? Or was I bowing my head down in defeat to the gods? My eyes started to swell and tears fell down my cheeks like a waterfall. They soaked the earth so much that oceans opened before me. I put my hands on my stomach and looked at everything that existed before me—my life, my world.

Kabir couldn't even make eye contact with me.

He silently wept.

I tried to dry his eyes as I wiped my tears.

"I believe I have always known."

"This was written all along, long before you even took birth. There is nothing, nothing at all, I could have done to change this. This was your kismet (destiny), the path you had to walk this lifetime. I did not tell you before because this would have shaped the way you lived: what you saw, what you loved, how you loved, what you gave, and what you felt. You would not have been able to let go completely if you knew death's date—and this life you have known would be unknown. The journey of love that you have experienced is rare. Many go innumerable births and lifetimes seeking and not attaining a glimpse of what it is that you have. One can only experience unconditional love and a life of no limits when they have surrendered their soul to the master of experiences within. Then one may freely dance with the consciousness of the universe."

Each tear I dropped into the earth released a memory.

I gazed into Kabir's eyes, past all the destiny lines and fine wrinkles—far past his universal wisdom—and directly into his soul. My words broke through my tears. "I...I want you to know something. I am not crying for such a fate, but rather for the blessings of my existence. None have lived like me. My existence was a devised planning. Truly, a blessing from the gods. What a gift."

I sat in silence until I was able to gain my composure.

"There is something I need to ask of you. Something that I know I should not, but I must. Promise me such a request. Your words shall never be heard by any other...ever. Especially the king. He cannot and will not ever know."

"Arjumand, does he not have a right to know? How can you hide your fate from your beloved?"

I gathered my nonexistent energy to assert my wishes. "Don't you see that nothing can be done? If this is my kismet, then what use is it? By telling the king, all I am doing is creating a world of death around him. And I see no purpose in that. It will kill him; all the while, I, too, will be dying. I must prepare for death, while releasing this dream I have been living."

Kabir stared in silence before walking circles around me, chanting prayers and sacred mantras with hypnotic incenses. He poured an ancient sacred temple blend over my head that would help to ease my transition into the afterlife. I came to believe in that moment that if the universe made up its mind, then so had I. Before he left, I needed to memorize everything about him. I grasped his hands, never wanting to let go.

I wanted to take our memories with me.

I needed him before; I needed him now; and I needed him in every afterlife. It shattered my soul knowing that after this moment, I would never see him again. He walked away and disappeared into thin air, just as he had come—like a dream.

The children and I ate a beautiful dinner on the garden rooftop. I didn't show any emotions that hinted at what Kabir told me. We laughed as they told stories of their day and who they became. I read them an ancient tale of love before they dozed off, kissing them on their foreheads. I cherished each moment, knowing that every touch and word henceforth would be one of the last.

I craved a little treat—something sweet, something to take my mind away. I wanted to unravel my mind and its thoughts, if that was even possible. I knew I had to make a contract with the gods, negotiating my life away.

Teetu was washing dishes. "Are you still hungry?"

"No, I just feel like something, but I don't know what." How can you express what you want, but can't have? How can you say *I'm hungry, please feed me life because I am dying?*

I cracked a meek smile.

"Can I have some ginger tea with some ginger cubes?"

"Of course. On way, my Maharani. Is your stomach okay?"

"It's fine. I forgot to say thank you, Teetu, for dinner. It was marvelous. The shahi paneer, naan, and dahl, well, you keep outdoing yourself."

I put my hand on my stomach and tried to breathe.

He smiled and gestured with happiness. "Well, Rani, we all know how you love your food, as well as how you like everything to change and be unique. As such, I must try new things to keep up with you."

"That is true. I do love change and trying new things."

But not all changes and not all things, I thought.

I sat on the balcony and watched as the day faded away into blackness. Just as there was the dawn of a new day, so too was there the dusk of the night; all within the same face, at the same moment, even when we cannot see it.

What if Kabir was wrong?

What if the gods changed their minds?

What if this wasn't the end of my journey?

What if destiny was rewritten along the way?

What if? Wasn't that the way of life? What if I did this or that, or tried this or that? You can't escape the endless questions of death's reality until you become the master of the mind. Then, thoughts cease to exist. The mind engages and creates a story out of a story. Death has no final destination, and the ego can't fathom that it, too, will experience a death of its own.

My body was tired from all my thoughts. A bath was poured and a wonderful assortment of flowers and petals were scattered. Even though the water was warm, the marble felt cold as I dipped my feet in. It was like walking into a tomb. The crescent moon tried to comfort me with her half-smile. I laced my hands over my stomach and started to cry. I tried to hold back even though no one was around, except my child within.

But I couldn't stop.

What was the point of this suffering?

My body would die, but I wouldn't. Everything continues. I must surrender; I must let go. This wasn't the end, but the beginning of a new destiny.

I submerged my body beneath the water and held my breath, looking for the moment when my mind became so still that it dissolved into nothingness, like it had in the Ganges. Above the water once more, I opened chapter two of the *Bhagavad Gita* and recited the sweet words of wisdom that would officially execute my soul in the end—giving and knowing that God held my life in his palms all along.

"For the soul there is neither birth nor death at any time. He has not come into being, does not come into being, and will not come into being. He is unborn, eternal, ever-existing, and primeval. As a person puts on new garments, giving up old ones, the soul similarly accepts new material bodies, giving up the old and useless ones. Lord Krishna, who celebrates life and death, asks us not to grieve for the body, for the soul is eternal."

I heard the door creak open and my beloved's voice calling my name. I dipped myself underwater to let the residue of my tears wash away. I could see him staring at me through the water. I looked at him through our transparent barrier as I came up. I automatically kissed him all over his face. I still don't have words to describe such a face.

"How was your day?" he asked.

"You first." I always wanted to hear him—to feel how he was, to know what he saw, and what he had done.

"Well, we adhered to the rule you created for tree preservation; everyone thought it was brilliant. But I told them it was not from me. All that I do is from my beloved, even when she is not here." He had a way of including me, even when my presence was absent. "I know you can't be there to advise; but when you are better, you will resume your throne of power."

I gazed into his eyes and smiled.

"Resume my throne of power...."

"Well, yes, my Maharani. You will be back after your rest from this birth."

My thoughts must have showed on my face.

"What are you thinking?" he asked.

"Oh, I'm so sorry. I was just taken away by you once again."

He placed a hand delicately on my stomach and glided his hands, like wings, to my breasts. He playfully bit my neck. I remembered how he told me a tale that when we were tigers, he would own me by the mark of his bite; all the other tigers knew that I was his, and his only. I arched my back in delight in order to draw myself closer to him.

I was so sensitive.

I wanted him inside of me; I would endure any amount of pain to have him, especially since death was on a clock. I stood up, knowing that he watched my naked body in admiration as I stepped out of the bath. I grabbed a cotton sheet and wrapped myself in it. My wet feet left little puddles to my desired destination on the bed. I dropped the sheet from my body and unraveled my hair from its bun, allowing the solar energy that my hair collected during the day to run down my serpent spine and cover my breasts with erotic modesty.

I could feel the heat from his skin as he gently climbed on top of me. The water from the bath dried on my skin, but it transformed into sweat from the intensity and heat exchanged between our bodies.

I was wet again.

He kissed me all over my body as though I was a work of precious art that he needed to consume. He ran his fingers through my damp hair and traced the curves of my hips. When he looked at me, all I could see in his eyes was a reflection of love.

All I could see in his eyes…was me.

I grabbed onto him for dear life, fighting the tears that started to well in my eyes—not from the physical pain, as he was ever so delicate, but because of what I knew. My heart spoke: This would be the last time he was inside of me. This would be the last time we made love.

षट्त्रिंशत्

I devoured death's thoughts in Sufi mysticism. The path of Sufism is passionate about death and proclaims the best way to prepare for death is to practice the sacred art of dying while you are still alive. I began to wonder how you really die when you're alive. I knew many times within my lifetime I died in the experiences I lived and took a rebirth, but now I was truly dying. It was known that in order to die, one must surrender to God and destroy the self before the last breath is taken. This act of contemplation of death is known as Ibadah. In the Quran, questions are asked about its meaning, such as: Did you suppose that we created you for amusement and that you would not return to us? I knew I would be returning to whomever I was destined for as I laid in bed in corpse pose offering love to God in the hope that I could attain fana (to cease to exist). Sometimes I could let go, and other times I held on so tight I wondered why I was even trying to attain such an absurd concept. But the more I practiced, and the more my mind relaxed, the easier it got— like everything in life.

As my delivery date neared, the cramps and sweating were so intense that even inhaling hurt. I couldn't exhale because every time I did, I felt as though I was dying. The bedsheets were always soaked, sometimes with blood. They had to be changed numerous times a day. The lower half of my body was completely paralyzed.

Blood ceased to circulate.

I couldn't feel my limbs.

Many times, I had to ask for solitude, as the pain was so extreme that I needed a moment to silently scream. I was given mild doses of opium tea to elevate my suffering, which I rejected more than I accepted. I wanted to be as present and centered as I could—experiencing my truth in my preparation for death. I still wouldn't allow for my pain to be seen

The king wouldn't allow another set of hands to touch me unless it was necessary—or Jahanara. He took to bathing me, feeding me, and reading beautiful stories as he brushed my waist-long hair.

I devoured every moment.

Wazir Khan told the Shah it was simply another complicated pregnancy and that everything would pass once the baby was delivered. My father and mother were informed of the complications. When they arrived, I reassured them that I was facing the difficulties of numerous births. I promised them that I experienced this before and that everything would be okay. I had to pretend as much as possible. I needed to believe what I told them so I was believable.

I had to wear masks to hide my truth.

My eyes watched in agony as my mother and father left my quarters, knowing that it was the last time I would see them. Tears internally dripped down my body; that's how deep my love was for my mother and father. It surpassed the ocean. It was endless. It ran thorough every cell and bone that existed in my body.

Practicing the art of dying revealed a truth to me: Everything that I gave love to wanted to be near me. Sher stayed with me, even though she was allowed to roam freely. I confided in her first; soon after, all of the other creatures knew. I explained how I heard the baby crying in my womb. They all knew what this meant, especially the ones who were mothers. I asked for my bed to be moved so I could speak to Ganesh. When I told her what was to come, she wrapped her trunk around my feet as if she were hugging me. Her tears dropped onto my toes, covering me in a pool of elephant tears. She couldn't even bring herself to look at me.

She just closed her eyes.

I, too, couldn't look her into her wise, sorrowful eyes.

When I was taken inside, Ganesh followed as far as she could to the palace doors, trying to get in by using her trunk to knock on the doors. I could hear her cries and weeping from my bedroom during the night—with all of the other animals joining in. I thought it would be easiest to tell them first, but I was wrong. They knew the words even before I spoke them, which made it excruciating and unbearable. Animals are so in tune with their natural instincts that they sense more and know more than humans. They live in the truth of their instincts and heart, in the silence of their nature without the mind's manipulation. When two energies come together in unconditional love, death of one is the death of the other.

I stopped dreaming. Dreams are for the living—just like desires. I learned that one stops being a dreamer when one becomes conscious, for they realize all is perfect as it is. There is no need to attain anything more. Pieces of me were reborn in ways that could only be understood through death. I slowly surrendered my attachment to my body and freed my mind. I began to imagine what I wanted my last moments of death to look like, so that when I took my last breath I was present in relaxation. So I could channel my energy, which I would carry with me into my future birth.

As much as I wanted to tell Kandahari and Teetu, I knew I couldn't. I wrote a letter of deep gratitude to Teetu, thanking him for shaping the innocence in my world. I wrote a letter of love for Kandahari, blessing her for who she was and thanking her for our memories. I wrote a letter to Kabir and all of my children, thanking them for guiding me through their hearts. Each of my animals received a letter. The last letter I wrote was to my mother and father. Tears fell from my eyes in gratitude for each word I wrote. The letter became endless pages upon pages and was barely legible once I finished.

सप्तत्रिंशत्

I awoke with a premonition that I was to give birth. I knew what that meant and immediately called for the king. The children snuck in and were sprawled all around me. Some had their feet in the air, while others had their heads off the bed. Jahanara sat anxiously by my side listening to my tale, knowing more than she actually led on.

It hurt so much to talk, but I had to. I had to breathe as much life as I could into every dying moment. "If what you see within is true, then even if the eye cannot see it, it is true. Like magic. It's like how you always see me, even when you don't. You know I'm always here."

The king watched and listened.

I stared deep into their eyes, into their souls, as I kissed them on their lips. I watched as Jahanara escorted the children out; they giggled like angels as they made their way out of the quarters. I knew when they walked out the door it was the last moment I would hear their laughter and that was the last time I would ever see them. That was the last moment I would ever feel their touch. My eyes never broke away, even when they disappeared. It felt as though my eyes could follow them. My heart shattered into pieces. I wanted to scream in rage for what I was being robbed of, but I couldn't.

I had accepted my fate.

I kissed the king and looked deep into his eyes, past this life and the innumerable ones we shared before. "I love you. I have always loved you. I love you more than anything I have ever known. When I was a little girl, I dreamt of you; and from my dreams, you came true. And now, here you are. The gods gifted me life for one purpose…and that was to love you."

I discreetly lifted the cotton sheet a few inches and looked down: my legs were turning a dark purple. Even though I couldn't see it, I could feel blood leaking and seeping inside of me. It had a metal taste and an indescribable smell.

"Please drink some of this. It will help. I promise you." He fought to maintain his composure as tears streamed down his face. I didn't have the strength to open my mouth to drink, much less for the words I spoke. But I couldn't afford to gamble away these last moments. Time was all I had. "There is something I must tell you. I need these last moments alone with you."

"You must rest. You are about to give birth. You can barely speak. You are not well, my queen."

"Listen to me…please," I pleaded. "If–if I do not say these things to you now, there will never be a time to speak these words again. And then what?"

He locked eyes with me in horror.

Immediately, he ordered everyone to leave.

I could feel the baby moving down the tunnel of my body, making its way into the world. It would be less than a few hours.

I conjured enough energy to slowly glide my hand over his. "You will feel me forever. You will have me forever. Even after I'm gone, my spirit will be inside of you—even when you cannot see me. Look inside your soul and you will always find me. There I shall reside. Just close your eyes."

The air turned cold and stale. Emptiness hung between us. He could smell death dangling in the air, not wanting to believe its presence.

"I could not say such things to you before," I confessed. "I don't know if it was disbelief or the immense pain I knew I would be placing upon you, my beloved."

"You are scared, my queen. You are not well. You do not know what you are saying."

I clenched the sheets with my hands as beads of sweat poured down my face like a waterfall. "Please promise me that you will take care of yourself and always know that I have only loved you. I'm so sorry that I could not tell you. I couldn't speak the words and create such pain for you. I know that you have always loved me unconditionally, every birth—so much so that you gave me your mind, body, and spirit. I will never know how to repay those up above. I could not have dreamed of more if I tried. Please forgive me."

The king frantically called for Wazir Khan.

I tried to shift my upper body to gain some comfort as I was told to push, but I couldn't move or feel anything. My body trembled and shook uncontrollably. The gut-wrenching sounds horrified those who were in the quarters.

It even frightened the birds.

The crow that perched upon Kabir's shoulders appeared at the windowsill. An omen from the trickster of death, foretelling that he would be the carrier of my soul to the "other world."

I could hear all the voices talking to me. I could hear all of the words, but I couldn't respond. I was now walking into the open gates of death. I released my daughter and I was gone.

Death and life, all within the same moment.

As my body laid in corpse pose, my palm opened to reveal a key. The key to freedom and incarceration—the key to my past, my dreams, my future, my world, my everything. Some say keys are the opening to the gateway of heaven, for they hold the power to allow the beholder to enter into the eternal life. I knew that I died with my hands open because I always gave.

There was nothing for me to hold onto.

The king hysterically shook my body in mad disbelief—then kissed my face, believing that I would wake. I watched as his eyes darkened and blackness took over when he banished everyone from his sight. He sobbed helplessly as he held onto my lifeless body. I saw what I prayed I would not see.

When I died, it was not just my death.

The king died as well.

अष्टात्रिंशत्

After my soul left my body, I soared around the room——I couldn't leave. I didn't want to go. It felt familiar to be in spirit form. They say that when you die, the spirit is so attached to the body that it tries to enter it once again. That was why Hindus cremated the body immediately. My body was preserved in a copper box that was filled with sacred ash of the Babul tree, mehendi, Kapoor crystals, and sandalwood while my burial arrangements were devised.

I tried to make my presence known: whispering messages in the king's ears, making things appear and disappear, anything magical I could think of to garner his attention. That was how we lived when I existed—in magic. But I forgot, I didn't exist anymore. He closed all the pathways.

I watched as the king diminished in every way possible, locking himself into depths of despair and isolation. His jet-black hair turned white instantaneously. He became a mere shadow of what he once was. His body, once full of strength and vitality, was now a walking corpse. He never even held our daughter. Kandahari watched over her and named her Gauhar Ara Begum, "the hidden gem." Jahanara desperately tried to console her father, but all attempts failed. Love is so powerful and consuming that it shreds you into pieces when you are without it.

It can turn light into darkness.

Day in, day out, all he did was sit in solitude in darkness, waiting for another day to pass. He tried to breathe, but his body forgot. Breath lives in life.

He couldn't look at the sun because the light caused him grief. He waited for time to pass so he knew he was walking closer to death. He knew he couldn't take his life, for the gods gave grace for the creation of human life and killing himself would have consequences on his karma and future lives. So, the king took his life in another way. He killed himself with his darkest thoughts. He turned his suffering into rage without a glimpse of sympathy.

Night after night, he watched the moon religiously as he spoke his endless sorrows to her luminous phases. The moon always listened, but she never replied. Until one night she spoke to him. She instructed the king that the time had come and that he unlock the chest.

I watched as he traced his long fingers around the shapes on the cold metal chest, knowing he was battling within to find the strength to open it. His other hand grasped onto the key for dear life, as if it could connect us to an eternal life; that perhaps when he opened the chest, I would appear just like a djinn. I could feel the heat rising in his body—even the temperature in the room changed. Sadness, rage, laughter, silence, tears: it was a blend of insanity mixed with the desperation of grasping onto sanity as he unlocked the lock.

He began to unfold the delicate pages as he made his way to sit on the edge of the bed.

Dearly Beloved,

Words cannot express what I truly feel within, for that is how it is when you are walking in a dream. Maybe that's why I painted you even before I saw you. Or Kabir foresaw your existence. There are no words or thoughts that can compare to the experience of unconditional love. And that is what you have bestowed upon me: the gift of undying love. I am blessed to say that I have found this rare gift of eternal magic in this paradise they call Earth.

I see as my time is drawing near that I am not letting go; things are just changing, transforming like nature. Everything has a cycle, just like the moon. Life, death, and rebirth exist concurrently in the cosmos—all within a moment. And that is why you must allow for our dream to continue. That is why you must be strong and go on.

It is such a paradox: You can be given everything, and then have it all taken away in a single breath—everything becomes nothing. The children need you the most now, more than ever. I beg of you to let them in, to be a part of them. They are a creation of me and you; our blood runs deep within them. If you want to be close to me, to feel me, be with them, look deep within them.

I have left you a collection of memories—hidden and dispersed. They are to be opened at special times. This way, my memory will continue to live on with you on this earthly plane. A love that lives far beyond that which is known, far beyond time. Far beyond that which is spoken, seen, and heard.

What I wouldn't give to wake up next to you, to have one of our laughing fits where we land in a river of tears. What I wouldn't do...what I wouldn't give...to touch you...to make love to you... to have what I once had.

What I wouldn't do...

Your Beloved to Eternity and Back,

Mumtaz Mahal

एकोनचत्वारिंशत्

The king and I shared all of our dreams. We decoded the mysteries of our subconscious to see where our unconscious masks hid during the day. To share dreams was to share your soul. I continued to watch all of his dreams. I knew it was the only doorway for me to enter into his mind, body, and spirit—even though he didn't feel my existence.

That night I placed a dream within his dream. I painted the most magnificent ivory and marble mausoleum—a jewelled temple in disguise. A vision that came to me from a beautiful fresco I saw on the ceiling at the Shai Qila. When dawn broke, the sun changed the breathtaking marble into a hue of ever-changing colors—from deep pink and ruby-red hues, to blue. When dusk settled, it reflected the brilliance of the silver moon and golden stars, like Shiva. A Shiva lingam stood hidden below, along with Hindu lotuses and Shiva's crescent moon. It spoke, "Tell me the story about how the sun loved the moon so much he died every night to let her breathe." Serene canals ran the length of the pathway, mirroring the forty-two acres of lush green paradise—said to be God's Gardens.

It would be where my life began with my first breath and where it would end: Agra, India. It was the epitome of love—

the magnificent Taj Mahal. Its execution and meaning would be a wonder that the world never experienced before; born of love, unfathomable by mere mortals.

When he awoke, he ran downstairs for the first time. Everyone thought something was desperately wrong—that he went mad—but he ran to the library and began to sketch his creation.

Days turned into weeks, which turned into months.

He was hungry for the perfect sketch.

Since it would be a rare and grand undertaking, he dedicated himself to finding the greatest minds in architecture: Ustad Isa, the most revered Islamic architect of all time; Ismali Khan, as the dome builder; Qazim Khan, a renowned goldsmith from Lahore; and Chaaranji Lal, a lapidary from Delhi. Beautiful ornate calligraphy was placed by Amanat Khan Shirazi. It was encapsulated in jewels with 99 names from the Quran to chant upon Allah. Lapis amethyst, lazuli, coral, turquoise, agate, tiger eye, coral, jade, garnet, and bloodstone were inlaid throughout. For eighteen gruelling hours a day, and for twenty years, 22,000 artisans and over 1,000 elephants dedicated themselves to the masterpiece.

Many lost their families, body parts, and lives.

When it was executed, I wished I never saw its completion. Though my eyes were bewildered in awe of its magnificent beauty, I didn't understand the meaning of this temple of love. It was a temple created from love, but those who placed their hands on this creation would never be able to create again. It was to be the last thing they would touch; as soon as they finished, the king lined the men up. Each and every hand was immediately sawed off. My heart was devastated when it saw a mountain of bloody hands. Some of the hands still appeared to be moving, trying to create. I didn't understand how he could bestow such a cruel fate upon them, considering the incomprehensible beauty they mastered.

The Taj Mahal was a tomb of tragedy.

Love disappeared into the abyss of nothingness.

The king became so frail and motionless that he was a corpse again. When all you do is wait for death in the physical world with thoughts of darkness, it comes to one very quickly. You might not die immediately, but your body would rapidly deteriorate—more and more with each breath and thought.

Jahanara sat dutifully by his side, serving her numb father in delight. He couldn't give her anything emotionally, for there was nothing to give. But he loved her deeply and entrusted her with the precious title of first lady (Padshah Begum), which I held. She was such a kind and loving Sufi soul. She sacrificed her heart trying to heal his wounds, not knowing that she couldn't reach him no matter how hard she tried.

He was gone.

No one was home, no one lived within.

The king was no longer the powerful ruler he once was; soon, he was overthrown by our son, Aurangzeb, in an alliance with his sister Roshanara. Aurangzeb sentenced the king to house arrest in the tower that faced the Taj Mahal. The king paid no notice, for he was there all along in spirit. When the time came, God granted his wish of death. He took his last gasping breath hunched over the barred window as he stared at the beauty of the Taj Mahal with Jahanara by his side.

I breathed my last breath.

चत्वारिंशत्

I t was time for me to go, but I didn't know where. I had no place within the casket. I had no place in the heavens. I had no desire to take another birth. I had no home. So, I shapeshifted into an eagle, the transporter of the heavens and earth. Maybe I did so in order to do as the Romans claimed: set the king's soul aloft. I knew the king and I would not be reunited, for karma had changed our paths. To glide my vast wings and fly higher than anyone else in the skies, except for the gods, was exhilarating. I was appointed as the messenger between the gods and those who lived below. Bringing consciousness to those who were lost.

All that existed when I walked the world was now in ruins or extinct. It broke my heart seeing empires of great love and the magnificence of nature shattered by destruction. It got worse over time. Nature constantly created and changed, reproducing its magic for man's sins. But man's desires and acts of earthly greed began to swallow the earth. Natural disasters and acts of destruction became Mother Nature's response to man's unbalanced actions, which seemed to fall upon vacant eyes.

I was getting restless. Something in me wanted to be birthed, to be channeled, but I didn't know what. Or maybe I did and I was too fearful to admit it to myself. But my spirit guides knew; they were devising a plan.

One early dawn my spirit council, which was comprised of an array of animal faces with human bodies, whispered to me: "The hawk-human said that I could no longer stay hidden." There was too much electricity within me for the ethereal. It was spoken by a half-wolf, half-human that I needed to go deep within and connect to the divine and become all that I am through universal consciousness.

A tiger quoted Buddha by saying: "We have come here a thousand times before. Who knows how many times more we will come back and who knows what we may come back as?"

The council agreed that my soul's purpose was unfulfilled because I hadn't experienced self-love. That was why I was to take my 649th birth. I argued with them well into the night as we sat upon stars, stating that love must be shared in order to be experienced. I asked why I needed to take birth when I had found the secret to life: unconditional love. Letting go of unconditional love was the hardest addiction for me to release.

I still couldn't let go.

It came from another, a feeling that I couldn't produce.

I was told by a cobra head—that slithered his tongue before he spoke—that the true depth of love begins within. I couldn't argue with that. I knew that even though I took innumerable births, I hadn't ascended to such a position of absolutism. Loving myself unconditionally was a state I hadn't entered. Maybe in moments where I felt wanted or desired, but not for who I was, when I was just me—without expectations, judgements, or desires.

The council began to chuckle and it was agreed that I was to be given freedom to choose my next birth.

I flew all around the world and watched many lives and tales. Some had riches, others had unique cultures; some had earthly love, others had vast life experiences, and some had the illusion of a unique blend of it all. I was given glimpses of how my life would play out dependent on the experience I chose. I could choose a journey of ease or one that held challenges, which would assuredly further my spirit into an evolved soul.

After searching the world, there was only one place I could find that would allow me to wear countless faces, costumes, and energies. There I would lead a life like no other; although I would have one body, many of the identities and talents I have possessed would exist within me. That complexity required complete freedom.

I sat on the ledge of the balcony at the Tropicana in Las Vegas watching my mother. Slowly, I began to take off my feathered costume. Letting go of my wings was hard for me. It was a covering I lived in for 350 years. I took a few deep breaths and flew into her womb. It was dark and cold. I felt caged... I missed my wings already.

It began as a dream within a dream in a world that most couldn't comprehend. Magic entered my source from my first breath, guided by spirits. Please let me take you inside my incredible universe. The door is open.

GLOSSARY

Arsi Mirror: Jewelled pieces with carved silver mirrors that reflected everything when looked upon. Many women wore rings so they could admire themselves when out.

Bhagavad Gita: A 700-verse Hindu text depicting the dialogue between Arjuna and his life guide, Lord Krishna. Tales of the journey of life and of how to become one with the soul and the universe.

Cholis: Midriff-baring blouse.

Chuppals: Slippers or flats.

Churidars: Variant of salwar pants; they are narrow and more of the contours of the leg are seen.

Diyas: Oil lamp made from clay for special occasions; from festivities to the remembrance of a lost one.

Djinns: Spirits able to possess human and animal form.

Durga: Warrior goddess whose mythology is based on fighting evils and those who threatened peace with goodness and dharma.

Ghazal: Poetic music with rhyming couplets and a refrain that shared the same meter. A poetic symbolism of loss and pain, and the pain one endured through separation because of love.

Hanuman: The monkey god of strength and energy. He was worshiped for his devotion to Rama and selfless dedication to the god.

Haldi (Pithi or Manjha) Ceremony: This is where brides were doused and rubbed in turmeric for luck, happiness, and love.

Howdah: An ornate canopy placed on an elephant's or camel's back.

Ijab-e-Qubul: Acceptance of Quranic verses.

Ittar or Attar: Sacred essential oil derived from the most exotic flower and herb blends. They were used as daily fragrances for baths or in sacred ceremonies.

Jali: Perforated stone or latticed screen with an intricate ornamental pattern created through calligraphy and geometry.

Jhuti: Ballet-like shoes that were made of leather or animal skin and had extensive embroidery in real gold or silver threading.

Kajal: Ancient natural cosmetic used to contour and darken the eyelids and mascara for the eyelashes.

Kameez: Traditional Indian outfit with pantaloons and a body shirt worn by men and women.

Kismet: Destiny or fate.

Kurta Pyjamas: A long tunic with loose, baggy trousers.

Lehenga: A long, elaborately embroidered skirt with either beads, shisha mirrors, arsi mirrors, or other ornaments.

Lord Krishna: Speaker of the Bhagavad Gita who lived life as a god on Earth, devoting his life to love.

Magni Process: Extravagant wealth and gifts exchanged from both sides of the bride and groom.

Maktub: "It is written," your destiny is spoken for.

Maulvi: Muslim religious leader or priest.

Mehar: Financial endowment and mandatory payment given within the marriage contract.

Mehendi: Henna paste with elaborate designs drawn upon the skin for symbolic meaning.

Mudras: Symbolic hand and finger gestures that influenced the mind, body, and soul.

Mullah: Derived from the Arabic word mawla, meaning "vicar" or "master." A respectful word for a religious man who is well versed with the Quran and religious law.

Nikah-nama: Sacred marriage and social contract between bride and groom in which they will recite Qabul three times (I accept) with two witnesses.

Peshwaz: Long outer garment that resembled a tunic (similar to a robe and tied at the waist); depicted animals and birds. Worn with churidars and a dupatta.

Quran: Central religious text of Islam.

Raga: Melodic notes in Indian classical music; based on traditional patterns and scales.

Sarpeech: Turban ornament made of rubies, diamonds, and other precious jewels set in gold.

Sarasvati: Hindu goddess of the arts and creation, learning, music, and aesthetics.

Shakti: The divine cosmic feminine power and empowerment with energy so fierce that it can move the universe.

Shatkona-Hindu Yantra: Represents the union of the feminine and masculine form. Also represented as Shiva Shakti (energy).

Sherawni: Long coat worn over a kurta with either pyjama bottoms or a dhoti (or salwar).

Shiva: The god of creation and destruction. He is death of the ego and old habits and forms as well.

Siddha: Perfected masters who have achieved enlightenment.

Siddhis: Paranormal, spiritual, and super powers achieved through yoga and meditation.

Surya: The god of the sun who was the source of light, life, and the energy of the cosmos.

Vishnu: Hindu god known as the preserver. He protects the Earth from being destroyed and has nine avatars.

Walid: Fathers or brothers who act and conduct legal represention for the marriage

Wallah: A person involved in selling something specific (fruit vendor, clothing, etc.).

Made in the
USA
Columbia, SC